CRYSTAL VISION

by Edward Flaherty
The fourth novel in "The Landscape Architect" series

A mystery beyond price.
Seeing is believing… but is that all there is?
Anton Bruckner tells more…
through his motet music.

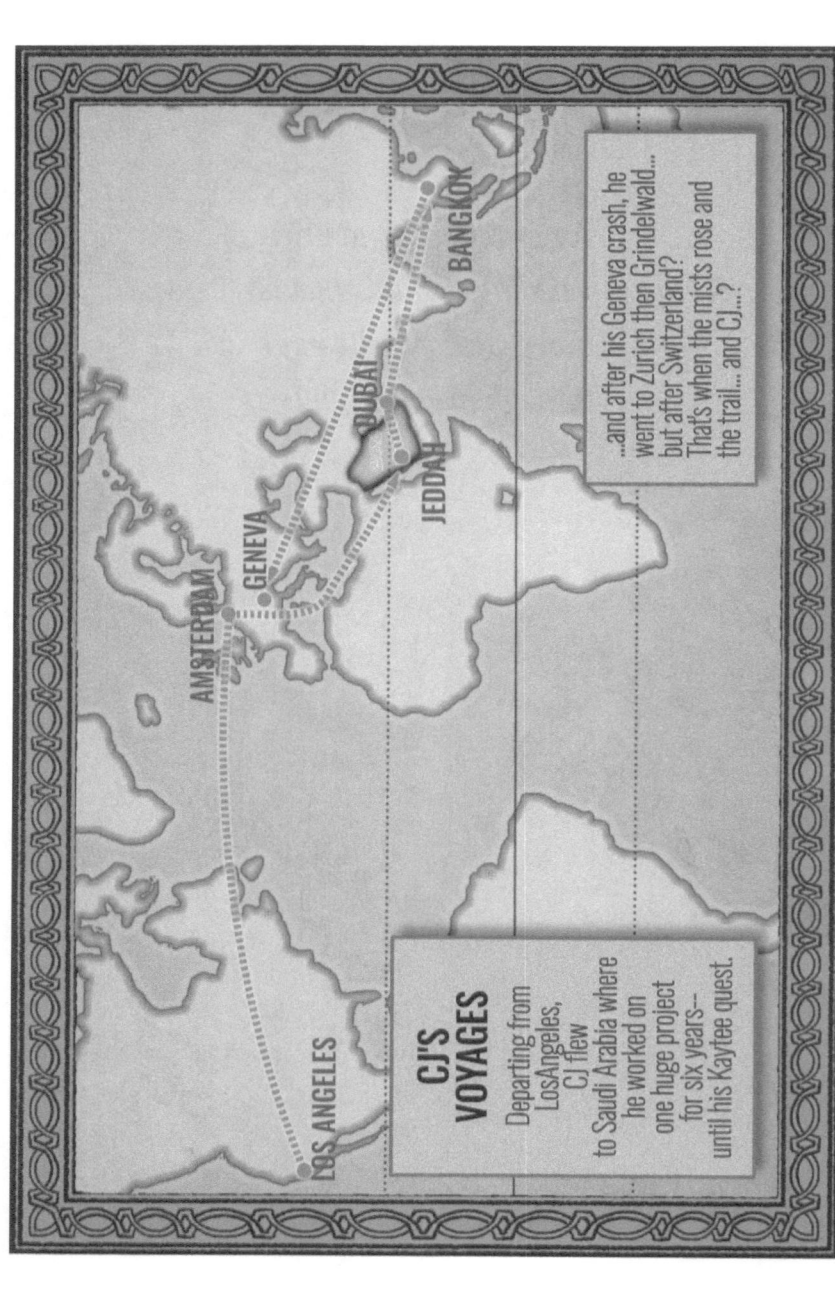

HIJAZ
MOUNTAINS

TIHAMA
COASTAL
PLAIN

Yenbo

Mangroves and
Coral reefs

RED SEA

**CJ'S
ARABIAN
LANDSCAPE**

Yenbo-40°Centigrade.
Salty sea,
sandy plains and
red ochre mountains.
Plants?
Mangroves and
coral reefs.

HELVETIA

CJ's quest for Kaytee ended with a shock in Geneva, Switzerland. But after, in the Alps, he experienced what? ... the "holy grail" of landscape design?

Zürich

Berne

INTERLAKEN

Geneva

Since 1291

Preface

Previously in *Tangier Gardens* and *Curious Tales*, Books 1 and 2 of "The Landscape Architect" series, Christopher Janus, CJ, our protagonist was a landscape architecture student doing a term abroad design study in Morocco where, with the help of a couple esoteric botanists, he barely escaped from an abusive landscape.

CJ then graduated, earned his professional licence and in New Mexico worked for years in design/build/maintain landscape architecture. But devastating personal events smashed CJ. To get himself going again, he joined W Kurt Milligan's Santa Monica California boutique landscape architecture firm.

SoCal (Southern California) has always been a design hub, the nexus of the "latest thing" in architecture/movies/television/media influencers and a small design boutique must be on top of it all. The professional design mood of Los Angeles, SoCal, is fiery—the competition is fierce. And so was CJ's relationship with Kurt—a friendship built on intense debates.

In Book 3, *Yenbo Palms*, CJ went to live and work in the Kingdom of Saudi Arabia where, for six years, he had been mystified by a landscape of chimeric sands. This fourth book, *Crystal Vision*, is narrated by Kurt who, trying to get clear on CJ's mid-career conundrum, follows CJ as he wends his way through an inspirational landscape into the unimaginable.

In the very alpine landscape that has inspired Tolkien, Byron, Goethe and so many other authors, artists and musicians, CJ absorbs the multi-dimensional majesty of Switzerland's Jungfrau Region. In those Swiss Alps CJ thinks he may have found the "holy grail" of landscape design.

I'll let Kurt, CJ's long-time colleague, friend and this book's narrator, set in detail the *Crystal Vision* context in his foreword.

Edward Flaherty

Foreword

In my Santa Monica Landscape Architecture office, CJ worked for me. He first worked as a summer intern when he was still a student. Then years later, after he was a licensed and well-experienced professional landscape architect, he rejoined for five more years. We were colleagues for over a decade. We became friends. We had bonds. He was an awesome go-getter.

Together, we worked with all the prominent architects and artisans in the Los Angeles area. We were absorbed in SoCal design, art and architecture. We were successful—a large part due to CJ's efforts. It was CJ who coined our office's letterhead and elevator hook: Irresistible Elegance. That's how we got on.

About seven, almost eight years ago now, when CJ, seeking much larger responsibilities, took on a new job in Saudi Arabia, I agreed to become his Executor.

Then in the last year, all hell broke loose. CJ died?! In Cairo? I couldn't believe it! I had to get to the bottom of it. The story? A never-ending wave.

Ride with me.

Keep your stuff together,

Kurt

Contents

1-Kurt   13
2-Zurich   17
3-Locus Iste   53
4-Blumisalp Stubbe   89
5-The Tals   141
6-Kurt In Cairo   203

1-Kurt

How We Got Here

...from Kurt...

CJ, Christopher Janus, took an international job in a developing new town on the Red Sea in Saudi Arabia. Before leaving for Saudi Arabia, he asked me to be his Executor—in case something happened. He wanted someone, a designer, to take his diaries and design journals. Me? I agreed out of friendship.

I admired CJ's fire. His cutting-edge design had done my firm well. Then eight years went by, not much happened between us. I ran my SoCal office. He performed his job in the Kingdom of Saudi Arabia. But CJ did send me, from time to time, twice a year generally, post cards from his R&R (rest and recreation—vacation) destinations.

Then about six months ago, I got a Special Delivery via snail mail from a bank in Amsterdam stating that CJ had passed away in Cairo. When, as Executor, I travelled to Amsterdam, I learned that CJ's death was an administrative declaration. Officials in Cairo had not found CJ's body. Yet, after a legally set period of time, six months, they declared CJ dead to clear their books. That shocked me.

I was sceptical. I wanted facts. I wanted truth. CJ had always been a source of energy and dedicated to the landscape architecture profession. He was a good guy—I needed more details.

As Executor, I emptied CJ's safety deposit boxes at the Amsterdam bank. There I found and took possession of his diaries and design journals. I began reviewing those writings and became stronger in my feeling that CJ might not be dead.

In *Yenbo Palms*, I pieced together CJ's activities through his departure from KSA and his quest to Thailand and Switzerland. At the end, CJ was in Geneva and totally bummed. I had never known him like that. He was depressed.

In *Crystal Vision*, I examine CJ's writings during his eventful time in Switzerland until CJ departed for Cairo. I have used CJ's diaries and design journals to clarify his landscape journey—and what a journey his time in Switzerland was about to become. Now it's time for CJ's own words.

2-Zurich

Geneva to Zurich

After a short tram ride from my hotel in Geneva to the Gare Cornavin, I found an express train ready to depart via Bern to Zurich. Just like that I was on my way. I was glad to have the frustration of Geneva behind me. It had hurt. I was at rock bottom. I needed... I don't know... something. My first time on a Swiss train—my first time riding through the Swiss landscape.

The mid-afternoon train was quiet, clean, quick, smooth, comfortable, not crowded. It had large windows through which I absorbed myself in the healthy outdoor panorama. The Swiss landscape is large, diverse in topography and easy on the eye. The words magic and spiritual flicked through my mind. Why? I don't know. I was weak and the landscape I saw felt healing. I thought more about it.

I had spent the last six years in a landscape devoid of water, devoid of soil, devoid of trees. Out my train window today. Water, soil, trees, green, spring. Magic. Spiritual. My eyes drank it in. I really needed that. Blue skies, nothing but blue skies! My senses told me one thing; but inside, I had nothing. The Swiss landscape nevertheless silently worked its magic.

As the train rose in elevation near Lausanne, I saw grapevines all the way down the steep slopes to the Lac Leman shore. I remembered the invigorating Swiss wines I had enjoyed in Geneva a couple nights back with Alex and Chandra after they had helped me find my suicided Yenbo best friend's ex-fiancée,

Kaytee. I thought about working with the landscape instead of dominating the landscape; but those thoughts were as empty as Kaytee's response—empty—nothing but an emotionally blank chalkboard—nothing. Then soft daydreams surfaced—half-conscious, half-dreamland.

My daydreams became a sketchy review of my work and living situation. My world was weird. I needed shelter. When I was RIFed (Reduction In Force, lost my job) in Saudi, that truly deflated my cocoon, my constructed cultural bubble, my personal emotional shelter.

I became untethered from the imagined stability of my work cocoon... untethered... my feet were no longer on the ground... I was floating... in shock. This was the first time I encountered the realities of large international project contract work. I'd been smacked in the face... no job... no plan B... I wasn't sure where to turn.

When my on-the-job, right-hand man and closest friend, Gordon the Canuck as I had called him, committed suicide in Yenbo, Saudi Arabia, I was shocked. Wasn't sure what to do. Then shortly thereafter, I was RIFed. I was without an anchor. I was lost. At sea, no land on the horizon.

I found some kind of temporary balance in my quest for Kaytee, as I was searching for her, the Canuck's fiancée, in Bangkok. I felt an obligation to tell her what had happened to her fiancé. In that way I was "closing the loop" for the Canuck—Gordon. It gave me some needed stability—even though temporary.

Then when I finally found and met Kaytee in Geneva... task complete... her reaction jarred me. Too much! She had already gotten on with her life—Gordon or not. It blew me away. I realized how important Gordon had become in my life before his suicide—how much I had been hoping for his personal recovery and success. The more I thought about it, the more I realized Gordon had become my guide, my signpost, my hope. How? Why?

Gordon and I both had disastrous personal losses in our lives—both of us had lost our wife and kids. I was always hiding from that reality—always weaving a protective cocoon around

20

me—professional and personal. It was an internal boil that never healed. In Gordon, I saw hope. If he could get beyond the loss of his wife and baby maybe there was hope for me. I was his biggest fan. But not to be had, Kaytee had just tossed him away.

For me the impact was huge, a multi-headed hydra—Kaytee's response, the impact from the Canuck's suicide, being RIFed. RIFed? This was the first time I had lost a job. To get that job in Saudi Arabia, I had cut many connections to the US. Emotionally, professionally, I was hurt. Exhaustion, emptiness and distress choked me. I had no job... no home... no future... I had an emotional vacuum. I was not sure how to deal with it.

Then the soft daydreams slipped away. I entered deeply into a dark landscape marginalia between sleeping and waking... a bad dream, yet threads of "logical" thoughts. I was in the company of my Saudi Arabian colleagues Bertram, JeanClaude, Alan, Gordie... they swirled around me like djinns in an Arabian sandstorm.

Then I heard the threatening Sahara screams described by Bree, a strange young lady who had shared years ago her landscape life stories with me one night in a Casablanca hotel. And the spirit of West Africa overtook everything.

West Africa? Those were the old days in Morocco... Aicha Qandicha, marabouts and too many unseen fears, too many unexplainable realities, too many West African roots—roots that still constricted me, my thoughts. Those roots always seemed alive in my dreams, despite the New Mexico Shaman's aural cleansing done years earlier.

So many landscape experiences, beyond provenance, had overwhelmed every thought and dream I had about landscape architecture design. I saw landscape as recorder of human culture—as influencer of human culture. Was it also a destroyer of human culture? Relationships between landscape and human culture... a realm so much larger than design. My dreams frustrated me. Unsettled, I tried to regain partial consciousness—partial control of my thoughts.

I had one straw of mundane stability... one certainty... my last duty in Zurich for my friend from Ban Muang, Vrndadevi—

21

return the Hermann Hesse and Thomas Mann books to her colleague. I'd do that.

On my quest for Kaytee in Thailand just ten days ago, Vrndadevi had alluded to the Swiss landscape as perhaps being the source of portals? And she suggested that when I find the true portal of transcendence, I might never need again a cocoon for hiding.

I was still tired. I became drowsy as the train zipped along...

Swiss landscape. Ban Muang gardens. Before I knew it, design took over my head. SoCal design—no permaculture there. It was an old cocoon. I approached design—planting design with utmost practicality. Planting design? My axiom was "right plant, right place". To this I added an obsession for maintenance to assure the health of every plant. That was the horticultural component to my design. But that was just a part...

I had based my core design approach on the basics of the sense of sight. My SoCal landscape architecture design work explored plant rooms. These were outdoor rooms using 100% plants to define naturally the floors, walls and ceilings. That is why the Ban Muang Obelisk Garden, essentially a plant room outdoors, so overtook me.

But what had most interested me was the concept of sequences of adjacent plant rooms. Connected sequences of garden rooms—each room like a chapter in a book. This had been my dream. For me, it was logical—it was the architecture part of landscape architecture.

Plant rooms. Transcendent Ban Muang garden room memories... Ban Muang? I dream-walked them again. Those garden experiences refreshed me. I remembered the best of my Hibiscus House lessons from Tangier gardens. Everything blended together without rhyme or reason—a carousel of sorts.

I gained full consciousness for a moment and recalled my youthful fantasies... imagining I could build gardens like the Oval Garden in Tangier and assure clients the experiences that lay ahead for them. The realities of paying-client desires and following government regulations put paid to all those fantasies. But for my own real-life experiences recently in those Ban Muang gardens—blissful—a cocoon like no other.

And then I fell into a solid sleep. I was in... barren—no plants—no water—the KSA (Kingdom of Saudi Arabia) Red Sea... mountains—my home for six years—a nothingness of ochres, red-ochres, drifting sands overtaking the buck-naked rock mountains. I squirmed and turned... restless and unsettled... something was missing.

When I woke, we were between Bern and Zurich. The train was fast. I watched the changing green landscape—chartreuse green, forest green and more green! I was awake in the bounty of healthy green and productive. Then I thought about my finding Kaytee and her cold-hearted answers—a solar plexus hit. Hurt and short of breath.

I thought about my cocoon in Yenbo. I could have carried on... the Canuck would have been replaced with a new Contract Administrator. And the new employee would have gradually erased the Canuck memories. I would have repaired the team and made it strong again. That part was clear... but... I couldn't get his loss of wife and child out of my mind.

I thought he had learned to live with it. He gave me hope that someday I would live with the loss of my own wife Sachy and our three kids—but now?

I should carry on, in his memory; I should carry on.

Looking out the window into the green panorama, I was re-energized by what I saw—the Swiss agricultural hill and forest landscape—moist, green, diverse, healthy—rich with promise and so deeply pleasurable to my eyes. Was I feeling their curative aura? Hope for my future?

*** *

Zurichberg

...in CJ's own words...

After a three-hour ride, my train from Geneva arrived in Zurich toward the end of the day. From the Zurich Hauptbahnhof, I grabbed a taxi to the Dolder Waldhaus, the hotel recommended by my Los Angeles bookstore friend. First time in Zurich! I felt the growing thrill of discovery.

As the taxi drove across town, I compared the Zurich downtown to Amsterdam, the town I had visited so regularly during my six years of R&Rs from Yenbo, Saudi Arabia. Like I had seen in Amsterdam, I saw in Zurich, through their decades, centuries-fine architecture, clear historical evidence of successful business. The richness of form, colour, materials and details told me about the proud people of the city and their gracefully dignified urban culture.

Approaching my destination, I saw the Dolder Waldhaus sitting proudly elevated, well up on the Zurichberg, a small mountain on the northern edge of the Zurich downtown. To my surprise and satisfaction, the hotel was not only adjoining well-established residential neighbourhoods, but also located on the edge of a dense, mature woodland stretching up the mountain. I liked the "feeling" of a rural forest landscape penetrating the city.

As the taxi pulled into the porte cochere, I noted that the hotel had the appearance, the feel of maybe a five-star in its day, but a strong four-star now, with its early 1980s textured concrete, solid modern architecture.

The lobby was quiet. The check-in effortless. I found my own way along the single loaded corridor to my sixth-floor room. I threw my case on the bed, opened the terrace door, stepped outside and breathed in the evening mountain air. Such a pleasure in a city, a dense urban area—didn't happen in my last two recently visited "big" cities—Geneva and Bangkok.

I relished the fresh cool air amidst nearby lakes, rivers and forest-covered mountains. I recalled how the strange, salty... the wretched Red Sea humidity, the lifeless landscape and burning temperatures that were my daily life in Yenbo, often felt like they were strangling me. Oh, was I glad to be here!

It appeared from the building layout that every one of its rooms, on all nine floors, had a south facing terrace... with a view of the city on the lake surrounded by mountains. The sun had just set. Below me in downtown Zurich and in its suburbs across and along the Zurichsee, evening lights softly twinkled.

The terrace, still holding the warmth from a full day of sun, soothed and calmed me. Far to my distant left in the clear evening air, the rows of snow-covered mountains were softly illuminated by the last rays of the already-set sun. The mountain peaks were beautiful, in pale, yet luminous orange tones, set against the dark blue-black eastern sky. A cool breeze gently swept across my terrace, refreshing me in its own way. I inhaled deeply and my lungs were happy.

Taking full advantage of the balcony terrace, I stretched out on the chaise lounge and thought what should be my plans going forward. A bit dishevelled from the shock of it all, I was still scrambling. What the hell had actually happened to get me to that point? I had completed a task, the quest for Kaytee; but, because of her words, I still felt empty and I had not yet fully escaped my Yenbo problems, especially... no job.

My running-around quest of the last two months seemed like yesterday. And the Kaytee meeting event of yesterday seemed to have lasted an eternity. I knew one thing for certain, I was glad to have finished with Geneva. The "close the loop" burden had finally been released. It was somewhere past. It had vanished around some corner that I could no longer see.

But I felt, in its distancing, it had left awkward emptiness.

Internally it still had an uncomfortable grip on me. When Kaytee showed herself to just be using my suicided friend who was deeply depressed from the hospital death of his young wife and newborn baby, I took a body blow. My own hopes for recovery from my disastrous loss of my own wife and three kids... those hopes disappeared with Kaytee's words. That was my new emptiness. My professional and personal future? Empty.

I stood up and stretched. Once again, recent events briefly took over my thoughts. They dropped in and I shuddered. Overcoming even the echoes of the recent past, the cool evening air—fresh and clean on my face—in my nostrils—began to purge me.

I breathed deeply. With my lungs full, my burdens floated away as unnoticed as an exhale. I thought, this had to be the mountain, forest and lake influence. In Yenbo, I had the stirring sands, their dunes and the Hijaz Mountains but... without topsoil, without plants, without fresh water... the humidly hot salty Red Sea air never refreshed.

Over the years, on my R&Rs from Yenbo, I had two special places for proper landscape retreats from Yenbo: the English Lake District and Scottish Highlands. At both of them there was some magic in the air. Magic that when I took a deep breath, I would immediately feel refreshed, recharged. That is how I felt standing on my balcony terrace, surrounded by forest and looking out over the Zurichsee. Fresh water lakes and healthy plant-dominated landscape must emanate a special magic. At least, that is what my lungs told me.

I sat down again, recalling why I came to Zurich in the first place. Vrndadevi had asked me to return the Hesse and Thomas Mann books to the Hare Krishna Temple here in Zurich. I'd do that first thing tomorrow morning, then look for Krauthammer, a bookstore specializing in design, art and architecture, one of the world's best, according to my LA bookstore friend.

I thirsted for those types of books. I longed to hold them in my hands. I would touch again great books, text and photos. These were the types of things totally absent in Yenbo. Tactile design, art and architecture things always generated fresh thoughts, new directions, design inspirations. They were my garden of new ideas. Dependable art and architecture bookstores had always been a large part of my repeat visits to Amsterdam. Krauthammer would be my test of Zurich. Tomorrow would tell that tale.

I looked at the range of brochures the hotel supplied to the guests. They were useful, filled with insights into Swiss daily life and history. I looked through each one and before long I noticed...

Night had settled in quietly over Zurich. The songbirds finally went to sleep; but, after I climbed into bed, my thoughts returned, about what had just finished in Geneva, and... what had not finished. No job, no home... and no cocoon? Finished, but not finished?! And deep inside? I was unfortunately still unsettled.

***

ISKCON Zurich

My worries and dreams disappeared as I fell into the deepest sleep. When I awoke the next morning, I felt the eagerness to explore, to discover the lay of the urban landscape known as Zurich.

I went online to find the Hare Krishna Temple. According to the online map, it was probably only a ten or fifteen minute walk from the hotel, most of it downhill along a brook within a forested green corridor. Before heading out, I checked my email, looking for something from my company, regarding the reinstatement of my job in Yenbo. Nothing.

On my way out, I inquired at the front desk about public transportation and found, as I had in Geneva, an economical day pass that would give me unlimited use and access throughout a generous central city zone. I had a couple stops in the central city I hoped to make. So, I purchased one at a transport kiosk conveniently located next to the hotel.

Displayed in the kiosk was a network map. From it, I saw I would have to change once to get to the stop closest to the temple. I decided to walk.

I liked to get the feel of the places I visited. And on foot, my senses could have direct contact with the Zurich natural and built environments. It was end of May, early June—peak spring weather, peak spring foliage, flowers and fragrance. The day? Sunny and calm, a walk would be fantastic.

Besides, Yenbo New Town and Tangier were both walking

towns. And recently Bangkok, Ban Muang and Geneva had been all about walking. I was accustomed to measuring urban areas by their walkability.

After about three minutes' walk, I found the forest corridor, the brook and the path alongside. The forested green corridor was no more than fifty metres wide, enclosed along both sides by rather dense, single and multi-family residential neighbourhoods. Along the path, daycare providers were walking groups of young kids. Nice little playgrounds were tucked in at sunlit and shade-dappled places along the way in this civilized finger of forest. In this beautiful, forested landscape finger reaching right into the heart of the largest city in Switzerland, I found the walk very pleasant, with no human threats.

I recalled my landscape architecture efforts in Yenbo, with its proposed green wedges of "natural" landscape, pushing in from the desert greenbelt around the town, part of the continuous network of pedestrianized, shaded, garden corridors. If Yenbo's green pedestrian ways could look and be used like this in thirty years, it would be a success.

In less than fifteen minutes, I found the Hare Krishna Temple street and was at their front door. Nobody answered when I rang. I rang again. Again, no answer. Then I saw a sign, reading, "Visitors please enter and take off your shoes". I entered, saw a shoe room to the right, and what looked like a small store counter a few steps in front of me.

After taking off my shoes, I stepped forward toward the store counter. At the store display case, I saw all kinds of oriental or Indian looking things. Ban Muang resurfaced briefly in my memories when I saw carved items and incense. On the wall, behind the counter, were shelves filled with religious-looking books, having covers with colourful photos of traditional Vedic characters, as Vrndadevi had described to me in Ban Muang.

Just then, from the above floor, quietly down the stairs came an older lady chastely dressed in a sari, just like I remembered on Vrndadevi. The sari fit in well in rural Thailand; but in urban Switzerland? I was surprised; but I figured it must be part of the ISKCON scene. She asked if she could help.

I explained, "I've got these two books from Vrndadevi, in Thailand. She asked me to return them here at this temple."

"Vrndadevi? I know Vrndadevi. She and I were in Ayodyha a couple years ago. My name is Laxmi. She emailed me that someone might be calling. Are you CJ?"

"That's me. Pleased to meet you. Can you take these books?"

"Sure."

I mentally ticked the last to-do task from my journey. Then, while handing the books to Laxmi, I said, "Please let her know that I gave back the books. Better yet... can you share her email address?"

"Sure, I've got it right here. Do you have a pencil?"

"Yes, just a minute."

Laxmi gave me the email address, then offered, "When Vrndadevi wrote she told me that you were fond of citron sandesh. Can you wait here for a minute, we have something similar—a snack you can either eat here or take with you."

I was willing and waited next to the counter of incense, carved wood, stone and brass oriental things. She returned quickly with a small paper plate of sweets—what she called burfee and halavah.

Laxmi said, "We have a guest room next door if you'd like to sit for a while?"

She opened a door to a room filled with plants, books and a couple comfortable looking seats with end tables. I couldn't say no. She led me in and offered me a seat and a napkin. Then she described the sweets she had just given me. She sat quietly with me as I sampled the bite-sized, enjoyable light brown piece of burfee, a sugary milk sweet, in texture like a soft caramel fudge.

I was surprised when she began to tell me in detail what Vrndadevi had written. She said, "I understand you have most likely completed your objective in Geneva, no?"

I acknowledged and asked, "How did you know?"

"Vrnda wrote me all the details. She wanted to make sure you were well received when you arrived."

I thanked her. She spoke softly and with a certain detached care. I wanted to get on to Krauthammers; but the sweets were wonderful and she was engaging.

She said, "Vrnda wrote that after Geneva, now is time for you to act appropriately in regard to your spiritual realities."

"What? What do you mean?"

"Vrnda wrote that you were seeking transcendent realities through your work with plants, right?"

"That's right."

"And we too seek transcendent realities. There are many paths a person can follow on this search. Didn't you and Vrnda talk about Karma yoga?"

"We talked about a lot of things—a lot of yoga."

"She asked me to elaborate on Karma yoga and answer any questions you might have because Karma yoga suits your condition in life."

Laxmi had respected me as a guest and I felt obligated to listen.

She said, "I would suggest you should make an intelligent choice about which activities to pursue in life. You could choose whether to perform your activities in any of three modes of material nature: goodness, passion or ignorance."

This had always been difficult for me to understand—all of material nature fitting only into three categories? So I asked for clarification. She answered, "Here is the essential background. The modes of nature are subtle forces that influence our behaviour as well as every aspect of our physical, mental and emotional world."

"Okay, I follow."

"The effects of mode of goodness can be seen when our life and environment are filled by an atmosphere of peace, serenity and harmony."

"Uh-huh."

"The effects of the mode of passion can be seen in lives dominated by insatiable desire for temporary things, a striving for more and more of them and perpetual dissatisfaction."

"Yes."

"And the effects of the mode of ignorance can be seen in lives dominated by laziness, depression, intoxication and insanity."

31

"Right."

Laxmi continued, "The modes of nature are defined in Sanskrit as ropes. And as ropes they bind us through the law of karma. Karma is uniquely human. For every action there is a reaction. It is cause and effect. It is based on the intent behind the action. Good actions bind us to good results. Bad actions bind us to bad results. As you sow, so shall you reap. It is a cycle of entrapment. With material actions, good or bad, they are all binding and continuous. The human becomes entangled and re-entangled—in actions and reactions—in happiness and distress—continuously."

This was going way too deep for me; but I nodded as would a gentleman who was following it all.

"Focus your seeking, your activities in the mode of goodness and gradually you will come closer to your transcendent goal. But you will still be bound by material karmic laws."

She continued, "But there is a way out. This yoga is a disciplined way to break that cycle and gain transcendental knowledge, transcendental experience, transcendental life. Your efforts, your work, your quests can become karma yoga simply by you becoming detached from the results. You need to understand that God is in control and the results are God's."

Well, now we were in new territory.

Laxmi added, "Karma yoga is very subtle; but your transcendent goals can be realized if you take on four personal disciplines in your life—no intoxication, no gambling, no illicit sex life and no meat eating."

"That's a stretch."

"Did you enjoy those sweets?"

"Yeah."

"Well, the idea is you have to taste something better before you give up something less. That is the first step on the best path in this age to reach transcendent goals."

"That's interesting; but I have to get going."

She still had more to say. "You might reduce uncertainties and tensions in your life by considering work as rendering service. You could then reach your professional and design quests in the mode of goodness. That could be your path toward karma yoga."

Her speaking reminded me of Vrndadevi—both with philosophically heavy words. Heavy words with peaceful resonance. The word, service, stuck with me. Do-gooding? Vrndadevi had spoken about service, if I remember correctly— true loving service to plants; but I was anxious to move on.

I said, "Thank you for everything; but I've really got to go."

We both stood up. Laxmi made a reverential *wei* and said, just like Vrndadevi had, "Hare Krishna, Hare Bol."

I put my shoes on, said goodbye, then walked out the door. My thoughts were elsewhere, my next destination, Krauthammers! I loved books, especially art and architecture books; and this store had been recommended by my old friend who, himself, ran a famous Los Angeles art and architecture bookstore.

***

Landscape, Art, Architecture

...in CJ's own words...

From the ISKCON Temple, I had to walk only two minutes to the nearest bus stop, noting, on the adjacent placard, the bus schedule and the central Zurich transport map.

Krauthammer, the art and architecture bookstore, was in Old Town on Obere Zaunestrasse, just downhill from where I was. Only a kilometre as the crow flies; however, the steep hillside roads were twisting, not through. I chose to wait for the bus. In five minutes I was in Old Town.

As I walked through Old Town, I wondered why, over the past six years, I had never before visited Zurich, the home of Dada, the home of classic graphic design, the home of splendid art and architecture. So far, everything I saw in this downtown urban core exuded high quality design. I loved it.

On Obere Zaunestrasse, I found the address, but... not the bookstore. According to my LA bookstore friend, Mark, Krauthammer's art and architecture reputation had long been established. Made me, in my landscape planner mode, think about the pace of change in urban retail areas. In Yenbo, for our starting intent, we had planned for a growing hierarchy of retail scales: local, neighbourhood, district and city centre retail areas. What might happen over time? We didn't know.

But here, even though this established retail area of central Zurich was bustling... change was occurring. Retail district shops change slowly—at rates sometimes hardly noticeable. Today I noticed it.

The shopkeepers told me it had just been bought by Orel Fussli and moved to the main street in Old Town. They told me I could not miss it. Right out the front door of their shop then the first left, then the first right. Then straight on about a hundred metres. It was a big store, easy to find. I found it in five minutes.

Bookstores have always been magic for me. Each book could be its own garden for me to explore. Magic, gardens, explore, discover.

Walking through the bookstore front door, I became like a kid on his first visit to a carnival! I looked around. I was in the magic garden. Architecture, art, design, photography, fashion, monographs, interior design, town planning, building construction, landscape and gardens. Tingling with excitement, I found Swiss-specific sections on cultural traditions, design, graphic design and architecture. So many choices, so many titles, I could hardly decide.

This was just what I had hoped for—big-time design inspiration. And holding these books in my hand—paging through them—impossible online. For me the Internet had failed to match that experience in terms of immediacy and freedom. Holding a picture book in my hands? Heaven.

I looked into the Swiss traditions first. Stamps, coins, Helvetica typeface. Then I found Swiss landscape architecture. And then I found my way into architecture and monographs. As I paged through a couple Frank Lloyd Wright books, I thought, it's funny what we forget from school. Every architecture and landscape architecture student must learn about Frank Lloyd Wright, Louis Kahn, no? Or at least they must be on the reading list!?

As I browsed every section of books, a massive flow of images and ideas refreshed me. From my hands to my eyes, to my thoughts, my imagination, my intellect. From these books, I drank in the Western cultural water for which I had so thirsted while in the Arabian desert.

In Krauthammer's, I had passed through a cultural portal. I looked at the Robie House, the Hollyhock and Ennis Houses. They told me the story of natural light, procession, sequence of spaces, the importance of the procession to the best view. They told me how to make inside and outside tell the most entrancing story, how landscape character and landscape structure evolve into architectural character.

While paging through these Frank Lloyd Wright projects, I explored the idea of a "view". I saw the view as a physical aspect of what I called garden "magic". I thought, what is this thing, "the view"... attracted to the view... a great view... it is something only seen with the eyes. What makes a view so spectacular?

Why is there anything good about standing in one place, looking out into the distance? Why is that good? Seeing and thinking is better than doing? Anomalies in a view? Or?

Is a view a guarantee of a portal into beauty? Or is it a promise of potential beauty? Is a view something that exists with value because of the viewers or without viewers? A view definitely has varying cultural parameters. And what do I see out of every window... a view. But views can be two-sided. Inward or outward views from any room... the garden room?

I saw in Lobell's interpretation of Louis Khan in *Between Silence and Light: Spirit in the Architecture*, that Khan built a design vocabulary and rationale around some real basics. Basic components essential to my own design aspirations for plant-dominated garden rooms—and the sequence of experiences moving through them.

Kahn took as his basics: sound and the absence of sound, light and the absence of light. He treated shadow as that chiaroscuro in life that can make everything simultaneously attractive and confusing. Both Louis Khan and Frank Lloyd Wright took the light from the landscape and created breathtaking drama inside their shelters, inside their architecture. My head swam with inspiration and confirmation of my own design as I read more about the works of these two architects.

I returned to the Swiss section and lingered, looking at those things Swiss—architecture, furnishings, joinery—seemingly so modernist, yet having an essential pragmatism, an exceptional application of craft. I loved their well-executed detail.

The morning flew by and when I checked the time, it was

already after one. I spoke with a clerk about Dada books. She showed me the section and suggested, "If you are into Dada, you must visit the Cabaret Voltaire, just up the street. It has Dada history back to Hugo Ball and Tristan Tzara. It is close, just left out the front door."

I thanked her for the info. I looked over some of the Dada books—art that is not art—and wondered about landscape that is not landscape. I thought the idea was a little interesting for not following social expectations at the time but, overall, it was not really convincing, a bit gimmicky... thought-provoking, none the less.

As I headed for the checkout, I remembered the Berner Oberland and went to look at geographically specialized coffee table books, like the ones I had seen in the Geneva bookstore. Here at Krauthammer I found many more books and in greater detail on the Berner Oberland, and specifically, the Jungfrau Region. I saw the art of Samuel Birmann, Ferdinand Hodler, and others, Lamy, Lory, Hurlimann, Mollinger, Konig—I'd never heard of them but their paintings and etchings... all were inspired by the Swiss landscape.

These were all new artists for me. I was overwhelmed, each piqued further my interest to see that strangely inspirational mountain landscape. These images helped build my conviction to visit those mountains, their snow, their glaciers, so much ice mass, so much water.

These natural mountainous frozen water reservoirs blew me away, especially so because I had spent my last six years in the Arabian Peninsula landscapes—devoid of water on the surface—devoid of plants. And during four of those years we had been entirely without rainfall!

Here in Switzerland, though, I found a surfeit, a surfeit of fresh, potable water. Everything was green, all landscapes were covered with healthy foliage. I had to look at the snowcapped mountains. That was fresh water, just waiting to be used. So amazing to my eyes was that surfeit of water held by the snow. Was that not, in itself, remarkable?

I needed lunch, so I went to the checkout. Under my arm I carried Lobell's *Louis Kahn*, McCarter's *Frank Lloyd Wright*. But along the way, something at a sale table caught my eye. I saw Sigfried Giedion's *The Beginnings of Architecture.*

I paged through a couple of the early chapters where Giedion unbundled the human internal existential uncertainties and repackaged them as a foundation for architecture. I liked Giedion's approach to architectural fundamentals such as shelter in the landscape; but the deeper stuff? I found Giedion's prose boringly academic, covering the same subject that Vrndadevi so attractively explained in her Ban Muang gardens. I concluded this was not really my interest now, put Giedion back on the sale table and proceeded to check out.

As I was paying, I asked the clerk about a place to eat and she told me that nearby the Cabaret Voltaire had a café bar inside, on the first floor. That suited me.

But I couldn't rush out of the bookstore. I had just touched again my old ways of inspiration, digging into design, paging through books, a long-term passion that had become for me an "oh-so-comfortable" cocoon of its own.

But I wondered, my landscape design passion... was it nothing more than surrogates for my search for meaning in life? Vrndadevi suggested that. My trip to the Hare Krishna Temple in Zurich did not rekindle my interest in the spiritual core issues that Vrndadevi had so eloquently uncovered for me.

But her questions had prompted my own thoughts about design having existential roots for me. That might explain how even when I finished a task, I never felt it was finished. I always felt an inner uncertainty creeping in... my own inner landscape unfinished?

I headed up the street for something real—lunch.

***

Cabaret Voltaire

...in CJ's own words...

After a short walk, there it was, just like the clerk said, Cabaret Voltaire. I went in, explored. Souvenir shop on the ground floor, narrow stairs up one flight to a café bar, and configurable performance gallery. Low light, high ceilings, lots of 1920s flavour, a few people, some talking animatedly, others sitting quietly.

At the café bar, I ordered a cheese sandwich and asked if they had any bitter beer. They suggested a bottle of Amboss Spez, a bitter beer produced in Switzerland. Sounded good to me. I sat next to an open bookshelf, open to the public, I figured.

I set down my Krauthammer book bag safely on the chair next to me, and started my lunch. Still thinking about landscape that was not landscape, I looked over the bookshelf and picked up a Dada book, Hans Richter's *Dada Art and Anti Art*. While eating lunch, I began paging through it.

Then something distracted me. Surprised, I saw somebody standing next to me, looking right over my shoulder... seemingly reading Hans Richter over my shoulder. Before I could say anything, the guy said, "Excuse me, you interested in Dada?"

What, I thought? This stranger speaking to me in English. In time I came to learn that my clothes gave me away and every Swiss person had at least five years of English language courses in the lower and middle school grades. He gambled I spoke

English. He was right.

I answered, "...kind of..."

The other guy asked, "Mind if I sit?" And without pausing continued, "Don't you find that Dada is bit of artifice to create some special node of energy? Maybe too artificial, what do you think?"

I looked up, paused before answering, and saw, a short, stout, friendly looking man in a red beret. He was about five foot five inches tall. Under his red beret, he had long, greyish hair, a tad stringy, free flowing, but kept, kept just to his shoulders. He was, what, somewhere between his late forties to mid-sixties, hard to tell. His clothes looked homemade, rough-cut, but nice. His boots were Raichle, an old well-known brand of Swiss mountain boots that I had read about, very well broken in, very worn, very well taken care of. But his skin gave no clue to his age. His skin did not look well-worn-by-nature or by the outdoors.

I answered, "Sure, sit down. I see what you mean... you might say Dada is artificial; but, in art, energy is energy... if it works, if it captures your attention, then it's alright. Don't you think so?"

The guy introduced himself as Ruedi, Ruedi Bärgli, from a small village outside of Bern on the Thunersee, and, as he sat down, said, "Yeah, but isn't that just a social popularity contest, whether it is accepted, within traditional society norms or, whether it is off the grid, so to speak?"

Before I could answer, Ruedi continued, "Look, I'm from Switzerland and there are places in these mountains that are natural energy spots... people have been experiencing them for centuries. Ask yourself a simple question, how did tourism get started, when there was no marketing campaign? People came to see for themselves, and they were convinced."

I was intrigued. This Ruedi guy had a healthy, fit aura. His handshake had been firm. His hands were rough like a craftsman, but not an abused roughness. I thought about Ruedi's comment and was not sure if this was landscape... or what. So, I said, "Tell me more."

Ruedi asked, "So, are you interested in the secret of beauty in these mountains?"

"Yes, of course."

"So, can you keep a secret?"

"Definitely!"

Then, with an almost comic finality, Ruedi retorted, "And... so... can... I."

I was puzzled and smiling at the same time. I was hooked.

I had just been riddled by Ruedi's funny little landscape joke. I was still trying to figure it out when Ruedi asked, "I have an idea... do you have an hour this afternoon, let's go over to the Landesmuseum, the Swiss National Museum. It's very close, easy to get to and full of interesting parts of Swiss life—past and present. Anybody interested in mountains and beauty is a landscape man... so let's go over there together and see how Dada compares with the Swiss landscape. It costs ten Swiss Francs to enter. What do you think, can you do it?"

I thought about it while Ruedi continued, "The Landesmuseum tells the history of the people who live here and their inter-relationships with the landscape, as far back as written history."

Before I could answer, Ruedi asked another question, "So, what do you think keeps humans from poking their noses too deep into nature?"

I looked at him quizzically. Ruedi, smiling, bounced up with the answer, "Bumblebees!"

Once again I puzzled, simultaneously smiling. This time I almost laughed aloud. This Ruedi had a certain jolly way about him. I chuckled, thinking about Ruedi's last riddle. Yeah, this Ruedi was a "riddler", a "jolly riddler"; and it all seemed to revolve around people and the landscape.

I thought, this looks like some good landscape fun. So, I agreed, "Yeah, let's go."

And together we left the Cabaret Voltaire.

***

Landesmuseum

...in CJ's own words...

On the way to the Landesmuseum, one tram and another couple minutes walking, ten minutes overall, I told Ruedi about my own landscape architecture background.

Arriving at the huge national museum, I first stowed my books in a locker. Then we entered and Ruedi led the way through the permanent exhibits. He showed the preserved rooms, dominated by wood carving, lead and stained-glass windows, painting and gilding from the Middle Ages. We saw Celtic metal works, jewellery from before the time of Christ. We saw the history of the Catholic Church and the impact of the Reformation even to this day, with Calvinistic emphasis on hard work ethic and conservative morals.

We moved through another permanent exhibit—children's playhouses and toys. Ruedi commented on the way people used to bring up their kids, when agricultural life was very hard. He compared it to today when many Swiss parents are trying to instil the traditional values of respect for the landscape and hard work, in the face of a challenging environment of instantaneous digital entertainment and flickering timespans.

Then we went in to see the temporary, current exhibits. Ruedi focussed on the growth of cities and related issues. We passed through exhibits on health, on the landscape, on the first rush of nineteenth-century tourism, and the successive tourism vectors.

Then there was an exhibit on Maximilian Bircher-Benner, the doctor who, in the late nineteenth century, started to address how a certain simple living with the landscape could cure the negative effects of modern industrial life. I recalled it was about the same time, the latter half of the nineteenth century, when Frederick Law Olmsted argued that the health of people in the industrial cities was undermined by the lack of green open spaces, the lack of places for play and recreation close to the home.

Ruedi interrupted my thoughts when he asked, "For what purpose was this world created?"

I was wondering if this was a joke or a rhetorical question, when Ruedi said, "This one is easy, CJ."

Then Ruedi answered the riddle, "For what purpose was this world created? To drive us mad.

"Actually," Ruedi continued, "I have to give credit to Voltaire in Candide, for this one. And this Dr. Bircher-Benner helped reduce the madness in our lives."

Ruedi emphasized the history of the Bircher-Benner muesli, the root of the omnipresent Swiss muesli so popular today, the soaked grains and the shredded fresh apples as the base for this first meal of the day.

He said, "At the turn of the century, Dr. Bircher-Benner met a German by the name of Ambrosius Hiltl. The two of them put together a healthy menu and Hiltl opened a vegetarian restaurant. Now, more than 100 years later, four family generations later, always evolving with the times, that restaurant has continuously and successfully operated here in Zurich. Are you a vegetarian?"

"No, not really, I've never been, what you might say, a grass and grain nibbler... but I have enjoyed some great vegetarian meals from India and I often eat Lebanese food which has a lot of vegetarian-type plates."

"Well, look, if you are going to be in Zurich, Hiltl serves both of those kinds of food, buffet style. They are not far from the Hauptbahnhof, just off Bahnhofstrasse, near the Globus Department Store. But watch out, Hiltl is so busy these days, you need a reservation at peak hours."

"Thanks, I just might check it out."

"But listen, CJ, let's get back to our original discussion on energy spots in the landscape. You have to get out of the city. There is a certain covering in cities... generated by huge numbers of people chasing, almost lemming-like... with passion chasing something, chasing dreams, chasing anything, everything! It is the chasing, the energy spent chasing. Dogs chasing their own tails... chickens running around with their heads cut off... that all happens when the ambition to succeed exceeds a certain level, the energy transforms... it takes on a negative characteristic, a negative charge, if you will... maybe you can call it a greedy energy... and that is what distracts, what dims cities. Too many people with greedy energy... ignoring the landscape sources and relationships."

His point made, Ruedi then asked, "Do you know why some people are working so hard to find a good balance with nature these days?

I was getting used to this now, and immediately, like the straight man in a comedy routine, asked, "Why?"

"It is like this—a rabbit was being chased by a dog. The people watching shouted encouragement to the rabbit—run hard, escape! And the rabbit said, 'For goodness' sake, shoot the dog!'"

"I'm not sure I get that one, Ruedi."

"People's boiling passion deadens their finer senses of perception. And a bunch of people, doing that simultaneously, generate a subtle, often not-so-subtle covering, or masking. Think about it. You have a bunch of people doing a lot of things, very intensely without ever thinking about the landscape, without ever thinking about how they or the products of their own energy interact with the landscape. They ignore the fundamentals, the elementals. If you look at the landscape energy quotient as a certain kind of electrical charge... the more people operating in passion, in ignorance of that landscape, the dimmer the charge."

"That's an interesting concept."

"So, CJ, look, head up to the Berner Oberland, Thunersee, Interlaken, the Jungfrau Region... it's just a train ride... see for yourself. Experience it yourself. See if the 'electrical charge' from the landscape is greater up there than here. I know the answer already, I live up there. But you, you as a landscape professional need to experience it."

Ruedi said, "Listen, I have another for you. What do cows, *lutins* (impish fairies) and men have in common?"

"Tell me."

"They all love the blumisalp. The answer is in the blumisalp."

"What is blumisalp?"

Ruedi exuded joy with his answer, "Floriferous pastures, CJ, floriferous pastures.

"So, when you get up there to the Berner Oberland, if the attraction is strong in a general sense, then you might want to actually get closer to some of the historical sources. One is the Beatus Caves, where St. Beatus, the first Christian in the region, approximately 100AD, made his home. Another is outside Grindelwald at the foot of the Lower Grindelwald Glacier, the Unterergletscher, a starting-off point for the overland route across to Valais. That should get you started."

I interrupted, "At the foot of the glacier, you say? Those glaciers have been attractive to me in the photos and lithographs alone."

"So go see them. And by the way, up in Grindelwald, stay at the Steinstelle, it puts you right at the foot of the mountains and the Unterergletscher."

As we returned to the entry lobby of the Landesmuseum, Ruedi said, "It is time for me to go. Do you know your way?"

I said, laughing, "I'm going back to the Hauptbahnhof to soak up some of that passionate energy. That train station is an amazing hub of human energy."

"That it is," Ruedi chuckled as we exited the Landesmuseum, "just cross right here and you will end up right in the centre of it. Did you like the Landesmuseum?"

"Definitely. Now I have some Swiss history, and you gave me a huge amount of enthusiasm to go into the Berner Oberland Jungfrau Region to find some 'real landscape energy'!"

I reached out, grabbed Ruedi's hand, and shook it heartily, saying, "It has been great fun. Thank you very much. See you

45

again some time."

Ruedi said, "*Schoenes tages, wiede luege.*" He quickly turned away, heading on foot back to the Old Town. I watched this strange character, with the red beret, the flowing hair, the lively step, the jolly riddles, disappear around the corner.

Ruedi Bärgli occupied my thoughts. An energy I thought might be like what I speculated was magic in gardens—a special energy? I'd been hooked. Strange guy. He told me that his name, Ruedi Bärgli, meant Ruedi of the mountains.

This fellow exuded a force that convinced me he was "plugged-in" to some energy source in the Berner Oberland landscape. I had to go see if I might find any "special energy" there.

Something about what he said made me think that good design had to derive its positive energy from the landscape. Yeah, in Ian McHarg's *Design with Nature* environmental analysis as the basis of design was a starting point, but Ruedi's take had a different dimension—his "special energy" in addition to scientific analysis.

I understood the Hibiscus House and Tangier gardens emphasis on maintenance; but Ruedi was drawing energy from something inherent in the Berner Oberland landscape. I hadn't ever thought about it quite like this before.

I had something to discover.

***

Bahnhofstrasse

...in CJ's own words...

I had just spent six years working at Yenbo Saudi Arabia—planning, designing, constructing a new town—residential, civic, retail and commercial. Now I was in Zurich, a new town 2,000 years ago, founded by the Romans. Today this is a mature town, working, healthy and bustling with activity. Safe and fun to be in.

As I inhaled the summer sweetness of the linden trees on the main downtown shopping street, Bahnhofstrasse, I asked myself, what is the secret of this Zurich central city success? It sure as hell wasn't those street trees—nice as they were. Street trees in the city centre business/retail district are like salt and pepper on the main course at dinner. Minor. That's all, an accent.

Made me think about my planting design approach. And what did I think? Sometimes plants are like cookie crumbs, like threads. Threads that can lead a person to the garden—the safe place where access to plant magic can be easily accessed. Small scale, personal, intimate.

But Ruedi, he had talked about the big landscape, the mountains—the Alps—the Berner Oberland—the Jungfrau Region; way far, a couple hundred kilometres from here. I was in Zurich. This was the first time and I was absolutely fascinated. I spent the rest of the day exploring the downtown core of Zurich.

The downtown core of the city centre was walkable—half

hour from the Hauptbahnhof, the main train station, down Bahnhofstrasse to Lake Zurich. Then another half hour from Opera House through Old Town back to the Hauptbahnhof. But a three-minute tram ride here and there made it an absolute breeze. I had a beautiful loop walk—about two hours with a tram ride or two thrown in.

What caught my planning/design/operation attention?

The Hauptbahnhof: Over 25 main national and international tracks on ground level with its easy, convenient and weatherproof access to regional trains and urban trams. At ground level and underground was a mixed-use shopping mall. The entire place bustled with people, tourists from everywhere, locals of every type. Nothing like it in KSA or even my own country, the USA. And the people? Everyone minding their own business. No one hassling.

A world-famous toy store: Something strange happened. I really had stayed away from toy stores since New Mexico, for obvious reasons; but this one was playing a jingle and the jingle was magnetic. So I went inside—four stories of toys. Videos, rest areas and snacks on each floor. But the message put me off. Message? Message was the aura of the store. Lots of interesting toys and videos but the aura in late spring was like the week before Christmas—got to buy now! It was suffocating with its pressure. I hurried out of there and fast.

Bahnhofstrasse hardscape/softscape: Fine texture asphalt sidewalk and street. Low profile granite curbs. Street trees here and there—lindens and their late spring fragrance. Tree wells edged in granite curbstones. Everything flush. No chance to trip or stub toes. Walkable heavy-duty treewell covers. Tram stops all had plentiful seats and well-designed signage with clear and complete information. Street for trams only. A very busy high-end shopping street.

Hiltl: That was the restaurant Ruedi had recommended. I was hungry so I went over. I went in and found a seat in a crowded, informal, café bar seating area.

The place reminded me of Amsterdam. It had the buzz and hum from a broad mixture of ages and types of happily social people. I enjoyed their self-serve buffet. I was happy to be there, happy to be in that kind of public realm. For an ever so brief instant, I recalled my segregated bachelors/families time in Yenbo, Saudi Arabia. The public realm there—it seemed... eons away... eons.

Sprungli Chocolateria on Paradeplatz: By its well-set out window displays, I had no choice but to go inside. I fancied a sweet. There, in discussion with the middle-aged saleslady, who was as neatly dressed and coiffed as the displays in the window, I was impressed.

She completed the picture of product design and customer care—clean, a pleasure to see—design and style and chocolate all one—very smooth but not slick, not commercial. A pleasure for the eyes; and, I hoped, for the tongue. Speaking with the saleslady, I learned of the worldwide reputation of Sprungli.

I do have a weakness for chocolate. I ordered 100 grams of their most popular—small balls of chocolate filled with ganache. They are called truffes du jour. Made fresh daily and sold out daily, as the saleslady told me.

It was about 9PM when I returned to my room. I opened my balcony terrace door, stepped outside, then after sitting down on the terrace chaise lounge, meditatively opened the truffe du jour box. I ate one dark chocolate truffe, paused to take the evening air, then ate one milk chocolate truffe. Nice, I thought, this was real smooth chocolate, a great way to finish the evening meal, the day; but something was missing. A good cognac. I called room service and asked for a Remy Martin VSOP.

I then took a long, hot shower. The cognac was waiting when I finished. I took the cognac and my remaining truffes, and returned to the balcony terrace chaise lounge. It must have been near 20°C. The chocolate was superb—made me recall that the guys from Tangier Hibiscus House used to come to Switzerland every winter for their absinthe-routine chocolate. Did they come here? I wondered, because this chocolate relaxed me every bit as much as the chocolate they served me at their Oval Garden—that was a blast from the past.

I relaxed, surveyed the twinkling night view of downtown Zurich, hugging the downstream end of the Zurichsee, and enclosed above by the dark forests of the Uetliberg. It was quiet. No traffic noise. My tongue was satisfied. My eyes were satisfied. And 20°C with no noticeable breeze, my skin was satisfied. I was comfortable, I was relaxed. Then I reviewed the day.

Had my toy shop experience been an Alice in Wonderland fall down the rabbit hole? Somehow that shop had strangely upset me. I had stumbled into something quite uncomfortable, and scrambled, to get out. Could Ruedi have it right about the covering energy in the cities? Then I thought: Something else... the effort, ethics and morals of the people who have lived here? I have always been consumed by landscape mysteries and this was another. The soils, the water, the climate and the vegetation were rich and refreshing. They were easily accessible and plenty of people could be seen outdoors walking and talking.

But the sociology of a successful central business/retail district—a proper mystery... and nobody can predict a sure thing regarding urban success.

I finished my last truffe, relishing the fullness and softness of the chocolate as the taste lingered over my palate. This city certainly had its pleasures. I had taken a good walk, visited the museum, a great bookstore, picked up a couple of classic books, every activity filled with the things that inspired my design thoughts.

Tomorrow, I thought, I could visit the botanical garden, and the waterfront of the Zurichsee, with its Henry Moore sculpture, its Corbusier building. Tomorrow, I would get more measure of this city.

As I finished off my VSOP, stirring images rose in my mind, the stirring images of photos and art showing Berner Oberland glaciers and mountains merged with Ruedi's descriptions of special landscape energy. All this was overlaid with my recollections of young Peter Camenzind's life in the Berner Oberland. These images compelled. They enticed me. They definitely exerted allure, an allure that pulled strongly on me. Without a struggle, I succumbed, and concluded that tomorrow I would cut short my tour of Zurich and take the train journey to Grindelwald. I would make those mountains, that landscape a firsthand experience.

With my last energy of the evening, I went online and made my reservation for, as recommended by Ruedi, the Steinstelle in Grindelwald. While online, I checked my email for an update on my job—my old Yenbo job that my boss Will Clendenon had told me might be reinstated. Hope, but nothing.

I stepped outside one last time, took the airs, left the balcony terrace door open, and then took rest. An ever so light, cool, evening breeze refreshed my room.

***

Kurt Says

The way CJ tore into his descriptions of Zurich—he was healthy. He was into his landscape architect game. It was the CJ I used to know. He always was an acute observer of how local people interacted with the landscape.

Interacted? That was how CJ described his perception of human social culture and the other life forms of the natural landscape. He used his perceptions of those interactions to develop design concepts for our work.

I hope to turn his Swiss urban observations into useful design approaches, like we used to when CJ worked for me. His observations on the high-end Bahnhofstrasse streetscape made me spill my coffee. Every downtown project we do is overdesigned with fancy paving patterns, as if that would make business/retail succeed. His observation turned that theory on its head.

He still had shadows from Kaytee but all in all, I sensed no depression. None at all. How could his shock and disappointment be wiped out so fast? Something cleared his head—the train ride from Geneva to Zurich? Zurich itself? The Swiss landscape? Ruedi? The anticipation of the Jungfrau Region of the Swiss Alps?

Whatever it was... CJ was back—big time!

3-Locus Iste

Angels we have heard on high
Sweetly singing o'er the plains
And the mountains in reply
Echoing their joyous strains

-James Chadwick

~

This place is made by God;
it is a mystery beyond price,
untainted by evil,
with extraordinary sense of peace and security.

Locus iste a Deo factus est,
inaestimabile sacramentum,
irreprehensibilis est.

-Anton Bruckner

~

Alps, An Introduction

...in CJ's own words...

The next morning, I felt like I was beginning something important. Discovery adrenalin—internal excitement. A fresh start. I needed that.

My destination? I didn't know what to expect. Yeah, I'd read some great novels, by Hesse and Mann, set in the Swiss Alps. I'd seen fantastic lithographs, paintings and photos from the Grindelwald area. They were all powerful. Then there were Ruedi's stories—he was convinced of special power in the mountain landscape of my destination—what was I to discover?

New landscapes... but my history with foreign landscapes? Not so good. Northwest Africa landscape had smothered me. Arabian Peninsula landscape had desiccated me. Now I was facing a landscape with such a positive heritage, such a positive recommendation. I felt enthused.

It couldn't just be tourist hype, could it? Unlikely. Switzerland? I had already seen in Geneva, in Zurich and on the train between them—snowcapped mountains always hovering in the distance. Large. Solid presence. Beautiful and powerful.

My InterCity Express train pulled out of the Hauptbahnhof for a three-hour ride into the Swiss Alps. Leaving Zurich at midday, off-peak hours, the first-class cars were almost empty. I sat by myself... dreaming. I thought about design and the books I had purchased; how Kahn and Wright both were inspired by the landscape, its light and its views.

From my window, I watched, between dense urban areas,

a procession of rolling hills, some forested, some in pasture. For me it was a time lapse sequence of spaces. Views always changing. Light always changing. Never knew what would happen next. It was fun. It was exciting—the close fit between urban and forest, urban and agricultural, agricultural and forest.

I was on my way, direct, non-stop, ninety minutes to Bern, the nation's capital. Bern, along with Geneva and Zurich, are the three best-known and largest cities in Switzerland—all densely populated and lying on the hilly, though relatively flat midlands of the country.

Before I knew, the train arrived in Bern's underground main station. I had to change to a regional train which would take me to the end of the line, Interlaken Ost—my first real life entry into the Swiss Alps.

The ride to Interlaken Ost would take about one hour with a couple stops at regionally prominent cities along the way. As I understood it, this ride would be into what is generically known as the Swiss Alps. Specifically in the Canton Bern these alps were called the Berner Oberland. And within the Berner Oberland, my ultimate destination was Grindelwald in the Jungfrau Region. That was how generic became granular.

As my next train left Bern, I sensed the beginning of a show. It started after the urban outskirts, amid rolling hills of mixed pastures and forests. The lowlands were filled with agricultural crops—no illegal tips. Nothing visually disturbing in the landscape view.

Little by little, I saw the entire large-scale landscape gradually expand its visual dominance into taller flat-top ridges, then to taller still, first range mountains. Each stage was steeper, showing more cliffs, until the peaks breached the tree line. I thought of this changing landscape sequence in musical terms as a promising first movement.

I stood up for a moment to stretch. I looked around the first-class carriage. No businesspeople on this train. In fact, I noted only one other passenger in the car with me, an older fellow maybe in his sixties. The fellow had on Columbia kit, not new, but worn. He had tanned skin, as if outdoors was more his way of life than indoors. He looked reasonably fit with a pleasant demeanour. The kind of guy who looked like he might have been here before, like he knew his way around.

Since this trip to my ultimate destination, Grindelwald, in the Jungfrau Region of the Berner Oberland, was new ground, new geography for me, I walked over to the guy. He was reading a *Geo* magazine, the French iteration of the American publication, *National Geographic.*

I said, "Excuse me, do you mind if I ask a question or two? Have you been here before? Do you know this region?"

He looked up, smiled, invited me to sit down. I offered my hand and said, "By the way, my name's CJ."

"My name's Ed, I'm American. Been coming here for vacations every other year for nearly 40 years now. If that'll help you."

"Wow! Yeah, that'll work. What do you do?"

"I do specialist consulting for UNESCO on issues of landscape culture and heritage in the Swiss Alps. It's been amazing, I work closely with the Institute of Geography, at the University of Bern on the Jungfrau Aletsch World Heritage Site. So, yeah, I know a little bit about the Jungfrau Region."

I filled him in on my own landscape background, especially my new and growing Berner Oberland Jungfrau Region interests.

"Here's the deal about the Jungfrau Region, CJ. The Aletsch Glacier is at the centre, over a kilometre thick and about 15 linear km of glacier. On this side of the Aletsch Glacier, it is all about the incredible treat of the three mountains, Jungfrau, Monch and Eiger. Where you're headed, they are the visual centre, if you will, the three kings of everything in that landscape. Can't miss them! And they're worth it!"

He continued, "When you arrive in Interlaken, you can get a view of the Jungfrau. Departing Interlaken you have to choose one of two valleys, Lauterbrunnen or Grindelwald. From Lauterbrunnen you see Jungfrau and Monch. From Grindelwald you see Eiger.

"Your ticket is to Grindelwald? That's the same destination

that I had on my first visit here in the 1960s." As his eyes glazed over in memory, Ed looked out the window and, clearly absorbed in an internal melancholia, fell silent for a while.

***

It Gets Better

...in CJ's own words...

Ed, well experienced from his decades in the Berner Oberland, said, "You said you're a landscape architect looking for the power of the landscape? Well then, if you don't mind, I think you'll find my original 1963 Berner Oberland experience something you might easily relate to on your first visit here."

Ed told me the story. "I was a teenager when my family brought me here for Christmas in 1963. I rode on the old trains all the way to Grindelwald—stood on the outside platform at the back of the last car, held on to the banister as the cog-wheel train slowly climbed up the valley. It was late in the afternoon... toward evening... overcast, grey and still. It was snowing. The ground and the trees were covered with a large-flake, wet snow—the snow highlighting the branch structure on every tree and shrub. Snowflakes were floating straight down only to be set dancing in the air by the passing train. In the narrow valley, the train crossed back and forth over the river—a river in greys and blacks—still flowing—in gentle rapids—with white snow to its very edges. It was the beginning of an archetypal Christmas... a dream then... a dream now."

I interrupted, "Forgive me, but that sounds like the *Polar Express* movie experience..."

"No kidding, I was in high school at the time, well beyond believing in Santa; but the experience found a special place... it still owns a corner of my heart."

I relished hearing others talk about the landscape. Remembering the snippet of *Polar Express* I had seen just yesterday at that huge toy store in Zurich, I asked Ed to tell me more.

Ed said, "A few years back, when I saw *Polar Express*—the snow flurries at night, the train ride through the landscape, the mountains, the lakes, the tunnels... then the towns and their warm lights—it was an old-fashioned déjà vu. The movie experience immediately reminded me of that 1963 Grindelwald train trip I'd taken."

"Which is the dream and which is the reality?" I prodded.

"Speaking of dream vs reality," Ed paused, his eyes glassy again, rather dreamy looking—then he shook his head, changed his focus, it appeared, and continued, "The reality is that this place is still as magic to me now as it was forty years ago—that's why I sought the job here and why I take vacations here—but back to the movies—the entire *Polar Express* sequence of Santa bells... where if you hear the bells you're carrying the spirit of Christmas in your heart, and, if you don't... well... here in Switzerland there are bells from church steeples, every day of the year; and every town, no matter how small, has a church with steeple and ringing bells. Then, if you're in farmland, the cows, the sheep and even goats are wearing bells when they're out in the pasture. If you take a hike in the countryside, you're bound to hear them—a kind of random mystical ringing outdoors..."

"Random mystical ringing! What do you mean?" I was thinking about Ruedi's words, "power in the landscape".

Ed ignored the interruption and continued, "There's even more here about bells. There are bell ringers—*trychler*, the Swiss German for it. They're people who take the largest cow bells and march through town for special events, special holidays. The large bells are very heavy and ear-bursting loud when rung. The men hold these huge, heavy cowbells with two hands, then march in slow synchronized steps, using their thighs, bouncing the bell, first on the left thigh, then on the right thigh, ringing the bells in unison. There are anything from fifteen to thirty men ringing and marching. They have their own mood, half-duty, half-trance. It's very impressive—demands a certain respect. It's a strange story of humans and cows and life."

"What's it really all about, Ed?"

"They ring the bells to chase away evil spirits. To chase away the spirits that might undermine the goodness and jolliness of the events underway, that's what it's all about."

"But where does all this come from? It isn't just about 'more cowbell', is it?"

"No, CJ, this isn't show business here. You need to look at the overlay of legends and history, landscape and the different peoples who have populated these mountains long before the Confederation of Helvetia was established in 1291. This is a place where roots from the earliest Celtic civilizations have never been 100% displaced by Christianity. After all, mountain people are mountain people."

Mountain people... independence... living with nature... we both sat back, and, absorbed in our own thoughts... said nothing more.

After a short while, Ed started up the conversation again. "Another thing that might interest you from the movie side. Remember the old Laurel and Hardy *Babes in Toyland* from the 1930s? The scenes of frightening creatures, called bogeymen, inhabiting dark places called bogeyland? They represented everything bad that could destroy the jolly, balanced life in Toyland. Well, their look, their costumes and masks were modelled on the same carved wooden masks that you can see today on old farmhouses. Right here! In the Berner Oberland!"

"What?! What?!"

"I kid you not. Even today, people come out in those masks at least once a year to 'scare' the young people, scare the kids into behaving properly. It's a very popular local event—many towns do it."

"This is all too coincidental, all too much, Ed. I just saw a bit of Laurel and Hardy's *Babes in Toyland* at a toy store in Zurich yesterday. And frankly, all this stuff about kids, dreams, toys... weirded out, I was just weirded out! C'mon, I'm just coming here for the landscape."

"That's what everybody says. But... take it from me. I've been looking at regional landscape ethnology for years. The landscape relationship to humans takes you to rarely visited corners of human behaviour. The human mind and the human spirit can lead to all kinds of strange discoveries—and stranger experiences!"

***

The Music Begins

...in CJ's own words...

As the train departed Thun, I could see in the distance to the east, over the Thunersee, a mountain and lake landscape interrupted by mixed showers and sunshine. The emergent play of the bright sunlight, the translucent greys from isolated showers in the distance, and the Thunersee surface itself reminded me of Turner waterscapes—that special softness saturating a dramatic, a stunning setting... evanescent shades of grey, each changing in opacity before my eyes... accented by sun highlights, the brilliant blue sky above and sparkling reflections in the lake... it was all alive... all symphonic instruments engaged. My eyes were hearing... music.

I excused myself from Ed and moved where I could have a window seat to myself. Sublime. That was the music my eyes beheld.

Then I got interrupted again. From across the aisle, Ed offered, "For example, today you can see there is a lot of moisture in the area. Well, these mountains catch moisture from the Atlantic maritime winds just like the Cascades and Rockies do from the Pacific in the US. These first ridges capture a lot of rain. On the lee side of Jungfrau and the Aletsch glacier, the average rainfall is about half, and much less dependable."

"...interesting..." I mumbled, barely getting my words out.

I was deeply absorbed in the small towns I saw dotted along the Thunersee shoreline. Each town had row after row of houses... not in lines, but densely packed clusters of chalet-type architecture, all with similar roof slopes and colours, stepping down the small amount of flattening mountain slope at the Thunersee edge. Uphill from and along all sides, these towns were tightly bounded by small, bright green pastures and large, dense, dark green forests.

Higher up the slope and further back, I saw smaller villages, dense with the same chalet-type architecture, also surrounded by pasture and dark green forests. Higher still on the slopes, in the rare bits of open pasture, were here and there, single barns or small individual chalet cottages, edged by dark forest or vertical cliffs. The higher up the steeper slope, the lesser the density of human shelter—respect for topography—a classic look of living with the land.

The chalets, the cottages and the barns all looked similar in shape, proportion, materials and colours, yet all had individual distinctiveness deriving from unique interactions between topography and building footprint.

The outer walls had dark brown, coarse, rough-textured wood with organically patina'd dark red and orange clay tile roofs... always it appeared on unmodified topography... almost as if the shelters, the chalets, cottages and barns had grown naturally where they sat. There was no hint of imposition on the landscape. And they all appeared to be comfortably aging with the passage of time.

I recalled something Hesse had written in *Peter Camenzind,* about a century ago describing the village architecture, "...built of timber frame in the old style... of no discernible age... a new cottage is rarely built...old buildings are repaired piecemeal as required... one year the floor... the next year a part of the roof... weak wood goes to fireplace or barn...". That is what I was looking at. In that landscape I felt a continuity that was large. Greater than human life. Not unsettling, but peaceful, restful. I felt relieved as I gazed upon it.

Then, revealing a parallel sociological overlay on the architecture, Hesse added, "...people who live in these cottages undergo similar transformations... each plays his part as long as he can...then drifts into old age... not that much fuss is made about it." I felt his words in the landscape. It was a strange mix I had never before experienced—a combination of the drama of a landscape in exciting change and a landscape calm with the acceptance of the change that death brings.

When the train traversed pasture and farmland, the proportions of the immediate landscape always felt small; nothing was supersized. The whole worked landscape was essentially human in scale and craft, even to the fence poles. They, of nearly the same diameter, were sized for easy handling, clearly hand-hewn.

Looking up the lake to the east, I saw, along both the north and south sides, ridge after ridge of steep mountains. One after another, they successively kneeled down to the lake edge. Way down at the far east end of the lake, I saw what looked like might be an isthmus—a low, flat piece of land, connecting the mountain ranges along the north and south edges of the lake. I asked Ed.

Ed said, "That's Interlaken at the far east end. What you identified as an 'isthmus' is actually called *bodeli*. It's a small delta that two rivers have created. Drainage from the north via the Lombach river catchment. And drainage from the south, from the Jungfrau Region via the Lutschine river catchment."

Ed continued, "At Interlaken, you'll find that some great writers and composers including Mendelssohn, Strauss, Byron, Goethe, Twain, Tolkien and many others have found inspiration in the Jungfrau Region. Some good and some eerie. Byron for example wrote his poem *Manfred*. His main character was up on the shoulders of the Jungfrau, in battle with spirits. They almost took his life... until he was saved by a local farmer."

I was in another world—not my home of the last six years— KSA, Western Region, Yenbo—no creeks, no rivers, no lakes, no soil, no forests, no scrub, no grassland. My insides became parched from the thoughts. I shook myself and looked out the window at lakes, streams, forests, pastures. I could feel the relief sweep over my body. What was I looking at? Wonderland? Dreamland? So much water, so much vegetation, villages that fit into the landscape.

Why not in KSA? It always felt artificial, threatening; why? Why did I think that way? No water, no soil, no vegetation. How could humans subsist? It was a pick-up-and-go place. Go to the water—go to the seasonal rainfall—nomads—bedu. Always on the move—never settled. Never secure.

But here, in this landscape, I felt comfortable, like I belonged.

***

Then It Happened

...in CJ's own words...

The landscape had been little-by-little occupying me more than Ed's academic insights. No big deal. It was all fun, but after Thun? Another world unleashed itself on me.

I became 100% overcome beyond words by a powerful landscape. Kind of like what happened some years ago in the Tangier Oval Garden. But then it was the beauty of individual plants in a small garden—here it was the large landscape. Mystery. Mystic. Magic. What was the force? On the day, I was so enthralled, I could not even ask the question.

Here it looked like people living in this landscape had made continuing generational commitments to their homes, to their landscape—living for the long run. The architecture of the village, the architecture of each individual unit had that committed feel. To me, it felt peaceful. In KSA the human villages, towns, encampments... they looked short term. They looked like they weren't supposed to last. I was preoccupied with those thoughts, when I heard a droning in the background. Ed's words barely made their way into my ears.

Without even thinking about the sky, I imagined this Thunersee as the floor of a unique landscape room—the Thunersee as its own movement in this progressing symphony I was in the midst of discovering... then... I was overwhelmed by the clouds!

They were dancing in the sky. The sky was the powder blue

hallway ceiling. But it wasn't flat. It was three dimensional...
no, four dimensional. It had unusual depth in that the blue
seemed to reach down from the sky to the very lake surface.
The powder blue sky transformed to a cerulean blue in the
water. And the pasture and forest greens, electric in their own
right, transformed into viridian green in the water. These
colour varieties interacted with the waves to generate motions
of rhythmic intensities. The colour vibrated with a life all its
own, rising from the lake surface, becoming adagio passages
in the atmosphere.

Without blinking, I saw this valley, at the same time, like a
gigantic, steep-sided Petrie dish whose purpose was to generate
clouds. It was a bowl teeming with atmospheric life... alive with
clouds... interacting with lake, with earth, with plants, with sky.

Clouds were at very different levels and very different types.
Long, loose bands of thin, grey clouds, maybe two hundred
metres above the lake, strung here and there, looking to be
in varying states of simultaneous growth and dissolution. At
the same time, higher and sometimes lower were puffy grey
and other times puffy white clouds either billowing larger or
disappearing. Then, in concert, along what appeared to be
topographic ravines deep below the dark coniferous forest
cover, were vertical lines of thin mists rising, on their way to
becoming part of the cloud party. I was amazed. I looked back
at Ed and he, too, after moving over to the lake side of the
carriage, was standing, mouth agape, looking out the open
window.

As the train snaked forward, the sun found more than
enough blue sky to shine brilliantly through these low clouds.
It magnified the whites, the brights, the light greys and the
darkest greys... blinding with its exclamation point brilliance.
The sun's power propelled shifting waves of greys, exuberant
cerulean blues and viridian greens weaving in and around
each other. I was inundated with energetic visual music. Not
for words.

Across the lake, in two distinct places, the freshly billowing
clouds had turned into showers... showers providing a
grayscale, evanescent, vertical wash over a small region of the

mountains, right down to the lake. But these were not like any showers I had ever seen.

The light grey veil of rainfall looked like some kind of direct connection for a high-tech duplex energy exchange... as much energy being returned upward, as being sent downward... energy going in both directions simultaneously... broadband energy exchange between the earth, the lake and the sky via rain and clouds. It belied anything I had ever learned in school, anything I had ever seen!

I couldn't explain it. But that was what I saw, what I sensed, what I felt. Some kind of energy was simultaneously moving up and down from sky to earth, and from earth to sky again... via the steady, gentle showers... without thunder... without lightning!

No sooner had the rain finished, when the broadband connection moved on to another area. As soon as they had moved on, at ground level the first strings of mist began transforming into fragile clouds which gradually rose and consolidated into long horizontal banks of billowing clouds. One bank after another, so that rising near to the mountain tops they obscured the ridge lines. The banks of clouds looked like multiple upper balconies in a concert hall.

The darker greens of the forest, the brighter greens of the pastures looked joyful... they were emanating a refreshment... the closest I can come to describing that feeling of refreshment was when I was a kid and really thirsty after a good, hard-running play outdoors... the joy and satisfaction of that first deep drink of cold, fresh, water quenching my ravishing thirst. I sensed that same refreshing feeling, that same joyous fulfilment, emanating from the landscape around me, the mountain slopes, the pastures, the vegetable, fruit and flower gardens next to the cottages and chalets... all fresh from a gentle mid-spring rain.

I saw it all in glorious action that day as I became a babe in toyland... helplessly enthralled.

What power existed in that landscape? I had no understanding, only awe.

***

Into Interlaken

...in CJ's own words...

The train stopped at Spiez. Ed, changing trains on his way to Milan, said goodbye and wished me well. I was only peripherally aware of Ed's departure.

I was under a landscape spell. My thoughts and senses had been mesmerized by my interactions with the landscape. That landscape had woven my thoughts into its ethereal cocoon. Ethereal cocoon? I... a strange inner joy... a fulfilment like never before consumed me.

I thought local human shelters in the Thunersee landscape felt right; and the essence of feeling right had both measurable and immeasurable components.

The immeasurable components of those human shelters, human habitation artifacts, had to have had some bearing on the glorious fullness of presence in that landscape that wrapped me up and swept me away. My challenge was to describe and define those immeasurable components that had the capacity to overwhelm human consciousness in a jolly—in a happy manner.

I thought my first Berner Oberland landscape experience may have been a larger scale version of what I had experienced way back in Tangier, for want of a better term, called "magic" in garden rooms. The plants do things. They do things to humans. They and the elementals, to use Ruedi's words, do jolly to humans. But the landscape? The large landscape?

As the train pulled out of Spiez, I was still under the spell of the large-scale landscape and its elemental components: plants, earth, rain, clouds, sky and sea. My processional experience though the valley and mountains continued.

I could see up ahead the eastern shore of the Thunersee, that flat known as the bodeli. The whole bodeli was behind a veil of 50% grey as the clouds had gathered and begun to gently release their rain, gently begun their energy exchange.

I looked back toward Spiez and Thun, and the Thunersee party of clouds and sun looked like a huge dance floor with everyone smiling and dancing together like an old-fashioned folk dance. I could only smile in wonder and awe of what was before my eyes. At the cloud party, jolly dancing!

The rain of connectivity I had seen over the bodeli appeared to be moving east, and as the train reached Interlaken, the rain had just finished. The sun's rays illuminated the entire scene, the entire garden city with healthy flowers everywhere. The downtown was freshly washed, and the air was freshly cleaned. All crisp, all clear.

As the train was passing from the West to the Ost stations in Interlaken, I saw, at first, three- and four-storey buildings right next to the track; nothing of the large landscape could be seen.

As the train swung to the north edge of the valley... then the view... to the south... the Jungfrau. Two steep foreground mountain faces gave way, somewhere in the middle ground, to two vertical cliff-faced mountains that narrowly opened to reveal the dominant shape, the snow-covered crown, the treeless sheer granite faces, the glaciated shoulders.

It was unmistakable, it was the towering Jungfrau... the view, somehow made open through the play of clouds, was a dazzling white snowcapped peak. And my pulse did quicken with expectation, with the hope of seeing more, of letting my eyes relax over the entire peak and surrounding alpine landscape.

It did look like a jewel mounted in the sky... and in a moment it was gone... the open view angle had been very narrow... I blinked and the view was gone.

The Jungfrau had disappeared.

71

At Interlaken Ost I had to change trains—a change from the regional to the local. The local would take me to Grindelwald. According to my reference, Interlaken Ost was roughly 500 meters above sea level and Grindelwald was 1000 meters above sea level. We'd be doing some climbing. It would be a ride of approximately 30 minutes. I had seen the Jungfrau as we passed through Interlaken. That was the million-dollar view. I wondered what I would be seeing next.

I had 10 minutes to board the Grindelwald train. Easy. As I settled into my seat I looked at my train info. SBB, the Swiss National train line, got me here. Now I was on the BOB, Berner Oberland Bahn, a narrower gauge, cogwheel local train.

I heard the whistle. The train doors quietly closed; and the train started ever so slowly, ever so smoothly. Quiet and smoothly efficient technology. Large and heavy technology made to feel light. That was Switzerland.

I found, riding through the Berner Oberland Jungfrau Region natural landscape, the brute experience of what I had once described as essential to garden design. A visitor must move through an obvious sequence of garden rooms, each having a dramatic play with light and proportion. I found that identical processional spatial sequence in this mountain landscape on this train ride from Interlaken Ost to Grindelwald.

I lived that journey as if in a musical trance. I lived in the flow of the landscape, as if it was music, amazed at how I was being manipulated by it. I struggled to capture its multi-dimensional reality.

If the Thunersee was a richly adorned broad hallway filled with cloud parties, then this next passage was a tight, twisting, secret passageway, barely large enough for one. I didn't know what to expect. Deep shade. Bright sun. Restricted vision. Open vision.

What next? All in a mixed forest of evergreen and deciduous trees. Late spring and the deciduous trees were beyond early chartreuse. They were each their own variety of spring green. And the evergreens? Still a healthy dark green. The trees, round crowns and pointed crowns, made their own music. The evergreens were composed, quiet, introspective, nonreflective. Deciduous leaves translucent, loudly celebrating the sunlight. Extroverts. I was fully absorbed.

And it didn't stop there. After the twisting secret passageway, I found myself in open, sunlit green rooms with views to distant snow and glacier-covered mountain peaks. I did not know what they were but I sure hoped I'd get to see them again. And I did get to see those mountains again. The distant view became a reality.

Then, there it was. Couldn't miss it. It was the Eiger *Nordwand*, for nearly a century the mountain climber's challenge, world famous for its sheer verticality. Oh, so high! Snowcapped. I could not guess its height straight up from the valley floor. It rose high above the edge of a broad, open bowl of a valley. Neither could I guess its width. The 100-foot-tall Norway spruces I'd seen all along this ride were, at the base of the Eiger, too small and too far away to use as a measure.

I saw, dwarfed in the foreground and middle ground, steeply rolling pastureland of what seemed like miniature farmhouses and barns. Fingers of deciduous tree masses led up to the coniferous spruce and pine forests which then continued up to the tree line or to the Eiger's massive rock face. The train turned and ran parallel to the Eiger, accentuating its long horizontal presence, supporting the great verticality.

All proportions and scale were severely dwarfed by the vertically dominating mountain. In the middle ground to the right, sparkling, little red cable cars, like bright red dots, the size of a single pixel, inched their way up the slopes.

Then I saw a train across the valley. I knew it was a train because I could see the tracks, aligned like a zipper up the landscape. The train of two or three cars looked so small... like an orange and green caterpillar crawling slowly up the slope. The huge-scale mismatches disoriented my metric abilities.

Then I saw two more mountains running east from the Eiger and in the same line as Eiger, equally massive, equally vertical, equally dominating the landscape, and I still had not arrived yet to Grindelwald.

The train engaged the cogwheel one more time, made its final climb and then we rolled slowly into the station. The mountains had been so demanding of me that, as I arrived at the station, I had no idea or vision of what Grindelwald may or may not be.

And, believe it or not, that was still but the prelude compared to what awaited me.

***

Court of Kings

...in CJ's own words...

I stepped out onto the Grindelwald train station platform, the only platform. One side to/from Interlaken and the other side to/from Kleine Scheidegg and Jungfraujoch. I looked around; it was quiet. I inhaled.

The air, thinner, crisper, had a cleansing cut right deep into my lungs—felt like a de-tox treatment. My lung lining accumulations from Saudi Arabia and Thailand were scrubbed clean away by the unforgiving sharpness of high mountain air.

I was finally at the base of the mountains I had been craving to see since the train out of Zurich. These mountains towered over me—merciless in their presence. They were vertical—all of them. Not steep—vertical!

The Hotel Steinstelle had sent a vehicle and staff to collect me from the station. We drove a short way up main street to the hotel. It was impossible for me to stop looking at the mountains. Checking in, I asked for a room with a view toward those mountains. They gave me a third-floor room. The Steinstelle was a sport hotel, mid-size, only three floors of rooms, where the expected clientele were fit, outdoors types who would spend all day (winter or summer) outdoors in energetic activities. The floor coverings were durable and made to be heavily cleaned, regularly. So I, as most guests did, took my own bags up to my room.

As I put my key in the door, I didn't really know what to expect. Everything in the build-up to these mountains had been extreme. In Geneva, the beautiful coffee-table-book mountain panorama images. In Zurich, Ruedi's strange mountain energy descriptions. Since Interlaken, the mountains' hide and seek mesmerizing beauty in the unfathomable distance.

Unlocking the door, then opening it, I was immediately smacked... those mountains were in my face!!

Big... stupendous... overwhelming... to the very far right was the Eiger... there was a narrow gap between the Eiger and the next mountain. In the gap was a narrow glacier-cut valley. I was so close, it was like my front yard and back yard all in one.

I could have reached out and grabbed it... if it was not so huge and ungrabbable! My breath was gone. I was hypnotized by its majesty. My bags didn't exist. The room didn't exist. I moved to the window, the balcony door and opened it... still breathless.

I stepped out onto the balcony. Overloaded by a real life cinematic, iMax experience, I seized the handrail with both hands, steadied myself... more than 180 degrees on the vertical... it seemed like 270 degrees on the horizontal as I slowly turned my head through the panorama, right and left... up and down. Large enough—too large? Weak in my knees—amazing.

I took a shallow breath... the sharpness had gone softer... and the air was sweet. It was clean. It had that sharpness, but it was a refreshing sharpness, softened by aromas from new-mown hay. I draughted deeply. I inhaled again and again, couldn't get enough.

I looked right and left, up and down at the details of mountains I had only seen briefly and from distance all day today. They were huge. They were complex. They were simply too much to take in!

Phew! First breathless, then speechless... a timeless experience. Slowly... slowly I came back to reality. I looked behind and saw my room door still wide open, my bag still outside in the hall.

On the Bahnhofstrasse in Zurich, I had nearly suffocated inside the toy shop, racing outside to find a single breath of fresh air. Here in the heart of the Berner Oberland, I was wrapped, I was swathed, I was bathed, I was being baptized in that fragrant, healthy, fresh air. I not only breathed it in deeply; but it, in return, infused every pore and every cell of my skin. There was some kind of purification going on, like it or not. And I did like it.

I tore myself away and went back into my room, grabbed my bag from the hall and began to get my feet back on the ground. I looked around, unpacked, sat down and checked online connectivity. It was good. I checked my email and there was nothing new regarding the re-establishment of my job in Yenbo.

My old boss, Will Clendenon, had told me that my position might be reinstituted, but no such luck. Might? Might be reinstituted? The reality is no job. Never been like this before. I might have to go out on the market—cold. Never even thought about that.

The reality of international contract work, I was realizing, was that I had better always be on the hunt for my next job. No job? That was heavily hanging over my head. I'd been out of work almost a month now. I'd have to go on the hunt now. But I was in some very powerful landscape. The Jungfrau Region landscape feeling touched me deeply. They fired up an internal flame of well-being. That overcame the dreariness of being without work. Hey, it was just a long vacation. And this mountain landscape? I've got to get into it.

I looked at the hotel brochures. They included a panoramic photograph of the mountains, with them all labelled exactly as seen from my balcony. From right to left, Eiger, Unteregletscher, Shreckhorn, Oberergletscher, Wetterhorn. Three massive peaks. Two glaciers.

My hotel was at 1,000 metres above sea level. The three mountains in front of me were nearly 4,000 metres above sea level. In real life, that meant they rose three kilometres, almost two miles straight above where I stood on the balcony. The mountains were literally in my face.

That evening I finally came to grips with the stupendous landscape procession I experienced—my breath-taking entry to the Berner Oberland.

I formulated some design protocol ideas and entered them in my Design Journal. I had had one hell of a processional experience that day! What was it... a train ride procession into these mountains... light, dark, shadow, sequence, views... and it all had to do with the landscape—the very-large-scale landscape. It was everything Khan and Wright had talked about, light, dark, shadow, procession to view. Lovely. Breathtaking. And again, pure landscape. I couldn't get enough of this landscape.

This processional sequence had an outline structure, in some elemental way similar to what I experienced in the obelisk gardens in Ban Muang—that is:

1. Seeing something attractive, something of promise from a distance;
2. Being forbidden to see it continuously; then arriving close to it, and;
3. Discovering a place of rest up close from which to explore it in detail.

And all this was exactly as I had speculated in my garden design axioms years ago. It was confirmation beyond doubt that I was on the correct design track. But how to make these happen in the domain of real-world business? I put it aside. Hunger had taken over.

My hotel had a small "authentic" mountain restaurant. The menu featured traditional regional evening meals, rösti, raclette, fondue, and the like. I sat down to a plate of boiled baby new potatoes, melted raclette cheese and a couple garnishes. My appetite was healthy. I washed it all down with a large mug of regional beer. Rugenbrau, it was. A type called Zwickel, unfiltered and pure like grandpa used to drink. That was how they advertised it. My thirst was healthy. I enjoyed it. I drained the first and ordered a second. Perfect with my raclette meal.

I stepped outside for a moment after dinner—to take the airs. Shadows of night had covered Grindelwald and streetlights, a soft sulphur yellow, were starting to come on. Everything in the street, the public realm, was built of wood, looked and felt inviting, comforting. I returned to my room. Looking out again from my balcony, I saw just the faintest orange sunset afterglow on the tip of the highest snow-covered peak. It was almost 9PM.

I commenced writing and it was not long before the Zwickel beer had its effect on me. Time for bed. I took one last turn out on the balcony. Night had taken over the mountains with its dark, quiet, very cool, even sharper, even cleaner air.

As my eyes adjusted to the dark, the mountains, emerging as a superhuman personality, brooded over me. They were a force. In this landscape, there was no doubt. They were the kings. And kings... everyone knows... have force, sometimes good, sometimes bad.

I took one more deep breath, looked around, up, down, left and right. Tonight in the court of the kings, all was well. I took rest.

***

Sixth Sense

...in CJ's own words...

The next morning dawned cool, bright and clear, with a light wind out of the northwest. I went down to the hotel all-day-dining breakfast buffet, had my usual orange juice, croissant and coffee, and headed immediately outdoors.

I chose not to walk back toward town, rather out of town uphill and to the east, nearby toward one of those landmark single-steeple churches. In five minutes, I arrived at the church, according to the plaque, established in 1835.

As I walked past the church, I saw on the downhill side, facing the glaciers and mountains, a large cemetery with a couple hundred small and tidy plots. The plots were already occupied, all nicely maintained, all healthy with flowers and dwarf shrubs. Each small plot had a grave marker—engraved stone. Each gravestone—unique and beautifully crafted.

In the cemetery, I saw memories of people. People who had lived and died in the sun and shadows of these same mountains. People who had been living here in this same place—in this same landscape over the past two hundred years or so. Those thoughts hushed me.

I took a seat on a simple but comfortable wood bench on the uphill edge of the cemetery—looking over the gravestones toward the mountains. Strange events were about to occur.

I was not in a built shelter, I was outdoors, just me and the ever-present huge and expansive panorama of foreground mountains... the Eiger, the Unterergletscher and the

Shreckhorn were aligned in front of me... waiting for my inspection. In fact, they were demanding my inspection. I was not in charge, they were bossing me. It was their patch. But it was all soft, all welcoming.

The mid-morning sun was warm. The sun graced the entire mountain landscape before me.

I was comfortable. From here, from there, sweet birdsong soothed my ears. My eyes flitted over and across the mountain faces, from one thing of beauty to another. My eyes did not long for more. They did not lust for more. They were just, unfortunately, incapable of receiving all the energy engulfing me...

The green of the plants fed my eyes a special energy... more than just images... what is that special energy sensor that people talk about when they say "look into my eyes, look deep into my eyes"... what is that? Well, whatever it is, it was being fed to me.

From above the treeline, the green ecosystem carpets, brilliant in the sun, burgeoned with an effulgent energy. My eyes drank the green energy from the coniferous forest canopies. My eyes inhaled the green energy from the individual deciduous mountain trees, from the pastures, from their grasses.

Then I had the most unusual experience. It was internal. It occurred somewhere in the back of my skull, maybe where the spinal cord joins the brain, perhaps an effect generated by the pineal gland. It was some kind of release of warm energy... soft effulgences... a soothing, warm release of energy in my head, filling my skull, flowing down the back of my neck, spreading over the tops of my shoulders down my shoulder blades... the warm feeling softly shut down both sides of my brain... it shut down all my senses... it stopped my mind, my thoughts, my conscious analysis.

This warm, soothing, pleasant flow entirely absorbed me in a singularly unique manner. Then after some immeasurable period of time, all normal power and functions resumed. Normal consciousness returned. Questions were asked. Assessments and measurements were made.

Prior to that experience, I was simply sitting on that bench, absorbed in the beauty, health and majesty of these mountains, the flow of water, the greens of the plants, the sun's reflected brilliance off the snow, the ice, the clouds, its exuded energy from the green pastures. What happened was not planned, was not searched for, was not expected. It was found, it was discovered, it was experienced.

A door? A window? A portal?

After I realized the strangeness of what had happened, I tried not to replicate it, rather to just live with it. I was afraid to try to replicate it... why... why?

Why? Perhaps the experience was too much like a psychedelic drug experience, perhaps I feared addiction to intoxication... or... or... perhaps, perhaps I had been granted, I am embarrassed to even think, perhaps I had been granted, as Vrndadevi had once suggested, access to effulgences of God and I felt nothing but the utmost humility for having experienced it.

This was a very powerful place. And I still felt dazed.

It was not a flower. It was the big landscape—the huge landscape! Somehow it had entered me... or... had it allowed me to enter?

Words, thoughts seemed antithetical—totally incapable of wrapping my experience. The flowers exploration in Ban Muang and the mountain exchange I have experienced here in Grindelwald both are garden and landscape experiences that I believe are transcendent exchange between humans and the plants in gardens and landscapes.

But I still do not know what that is! Even after having had the experiences!!! How can that be designed and built?! I can't even define it. If I remember, this was exactly what Tolly and Fyodor were after in Tangier. I didn't get it then and I didn't get it here. I took a deep breath and sat quietly on the bench for the longest time.

This Berner Oberland experience, this non-stop landscape experience on the train from Bern to Interlaken and on to Grindelwald... then on foot here in Grindelwald... this nonstop procession was a musical experience, a musical trance where

I rode the music, the landscape music for hours. It was a procession far more intense than I had imagined from Ruedi's description of landscape energy. It was one of those things you have to feel for it to be true.

This landscape mystified me. It captured and captivated me. What are the roots of this landscape? I needed to discover more!

***

Local Zwerg

...in CJ's own words...

I finally stood up and walked downhill looking at the gravestones and then back uphill toward the church—death and life all about me. There was a section of gravestones for those who, on the mountains, lost their lives; *bergfuhrers*, they are called, masters of the mountains, people who climbed every vertical inch of the mountains, people with intimate knowledge of those mountain landscapes. I sat on another nearby wooden bench. As I was looking at these gravestones, another person entered the cemetery, walking in my direction. I looked him over.

This guy was maybe my age, a bit younger, on the short side, maybe five foot eight, stronger-than-wiry looking, a bit rough, but clean. He had brown curly hair, not too long, and a full curly beard, also not too long. Shorts, hiking boots, heavy socks rolled down, sweater, vest, small but obviously well-used rucksack, and a stout walking stick. The skin on his face, hands and legs was all the same outdoors colour, weathered from being a long-time, year-round, outdoor person.

The guy paused for a couple minutes at a gravestone. I continued to watch. He turned toward me. Our eyes met. He nodded. I nodded back. The guy walked over and spoke English, or should I say Scottish.

"I beg your pardon?" I didn't understand a word he said the first time.

The stranger rephrased, "What do you think of this place?"

84

I answered, "This is one powerful place."

He replied with force, "No shit, Sherlock, is that why you came here?"

"I suppose so, but it's more powerful than I ever imagined. I was just looking for unique landscapes; but this place is beyond words."

"I have words for it. I respect it and I don't like the inundation of disrespectful tourists. The passion of their cars running down main street... it consumerizes, it commoditizes the mountains. For certain kinds of tourists this place is just another window of time to schedule on their 'crackberries'.

"What this place really is... is a place of pilgrimage... a place to get in touch with that part of us that a city dulls, dims, erases. We don't get many like you, sitting in the quiet, at the feet of the mountains. You have relatives in this cemetery?"

"No, but I feel just as though I'm sitting in a pew of the most beautiful church I could imagine. Sitting here in front of these mountains, I feel like... like I'm in the presence of God; and these mountains are communicating directly, without words, to some part of me that I never knew existed."

"Like I was saying, we don't get many visitors here, taking the time to receive the good that is available... the hope... the beauty...

"Mind if I sit down?" He sat down next to me. We both sat quietly looking out toward the Unterergletscher. Silence, we both lived it.

After a few minutes I asked, "You look like a hiker. I'm a landscape architect. I'm trying to get a grip on these mountains—they do something to me. I don't really know what it is. Any ideas?"

The guy replied, "Do you like to hike? If so, we can walk up that Unterergletscher into a really special place in that landscape, look a little deeper inside. By the way, my name is Ian, Ian McCloud, from Portree originally, Isle of Skye. I've been here working in a bakery for the past eight years; and this mountain landscape is bigger than anything imaginable. I know a wee thing or two about landscape around here.

"I make a walk, I call it the Malahide, to an ancient energy source where the Unterergletscher emerges between the Eiger and the Shreck. If you can make it, meet me at 5AM the day after tomorrow, my day off, Friday, in front of Ringgenberg Bakery. We'll spend the morning hiking on good paths, no real bergwegs."

He continued, "You got boots or good shoes? Never mind, you look like a US size 9-9½ , I've got extra pairs. How about it? Bakery's on the main street, right hand side, halfway to the train station, about ten minutes from here. On the day, we'll be back about 3PM. Are you in?"

I had doubts, this guy was a stranger; but I stuck out my hand, and said, "I'm in. My name's CJ. I'm staying at the Steinstelle; and I'll see you at the bakery, the day after tomorrow. Fair enough?"

"Good stuff, CJ. I have boots and heavy socks I can lend to you on the day. Got to go now. See you day after tomorrow at 5AM, got that, in front of Ringgenberg's!" Then turning on his heel, Ian left the cemetery.

I continued sitting. I needed to take a moment in the cemetery to review just what the heck had happened. My intimate effulgences exchange with the mountain landscape. My meeting with Ian. My scheduled hike to the Unterergletscher.

I sat for a quiet while. What captured my thoughts most was the mysterious experience that had grasped me internally. I had had my insides opened by the mountain landscape and I did not know how.

The landscape—this landscape—seemed alive and in another dimension—something I never before imagined. Time to go back to the hotel to do some serious writing.

***

Kurt Says

CJ's writing mesmerized me. He took me along with him into the Jungfrau Region. Two things stood out. He was enlivened in that landscape. He was not a candidate for suicide.

But there was something else. His train ride from Interlaken to Grindelwald, his cemetery/mountain experience—for the first time I was hooked. The large landscape was driving his design thoughts.

I felt through his writing that CJ had embarked on landscape perceptions that might link to what the two of us always searched—a larger, more powerful concept to apply to smaller scale landscape design. He just might be onto something. I was stoked. I wanted more.

4-Blumisalp Stubbe

There is in life, an element of elfin coincidence
which people,
reckoning on the prosaic, may miss.

--GK Chesterton

Landscape Music

...in CJ's own words...

Back in my hotel room that afternoon, I wrote with a passion I have rarely felt. The landscape experience I had absorbed from those mountains possessed me. I thought, okay, I've felt the power. It must be that power that Ruedi described. I felt it but I could not understand it. Then I met Ian. Ian spoke like he was a local landscape insider, an initiate. My walk with him up to a glacier may likely help me discover the hidden essence in this landscape—the root of its deep inspiration.

I've always loved exploring design and what may be woven into design. I had just experienced thick threads, streams of landscape experience the likes of which I had never encountered in school, in Los Angeles, in Saudi Arabia. Something more than external objects of the senses, something more than imagination, something more than emotional or intellectual constructs, something I had never experienced in church. The only thing I could relate it to were those odd experiences I had with plants in Tangier, in Ban Muang; but...

I tried to come to grips with the effect of these mountains. Vrndadevi had talked about the powerful impact of the Swiss Alps on great writers like Hesse and Mann. Now, I had firsthand experience.

I tried to outline my effulgent experience in the cemetery by subdividing it into four layers: physical, emotional, intellectual and spiritual. I speculated each of these individual layers could be absorbed from the landscape.

There must be special times when all four of these are simultaneously active and when so, they unlock doors of perception that reveal some kind of calming, pleasant, internalized experience. That, when I was observing flowers in my Tangier and Ban Muang gardens, I called "magic". Now with the intensity I had felt in this large landscape, these may rightfully be transcendent windows on effulgences—other-world experiences—all layers intensely active simultaneously?

Analyzing Tangier, Ban Muang and these mountains together, I noted that those internalized other-world realities occurred only when I lost the ability to distinguish the individual identities and awareness of those four layers of experience—physical, emotional, intellectual and spiritual.

Losing contact with time, space, gross and subtle senses... was that religious? Was that about a perception of the God? Could it be designable? I had to rethink that whole bit about religion and spiritual... because there does appear to be something out there beyond my physical, emotion and intellectual layers of consciousness...

I still had plenty to do.

I could say one thing only with certainty. I felt right investigating landscape, investigating design. My investigations took me to my roots. I continued writing.

I did not realize the sun had set. Dark erased the outside. I didn't notice. I continued to write. My stomach reminded and reminded. Finally, I paused.

I stood up, stretched, decided to take a walk outside back down toward the center of town. The evening air was sharp and cool. It was quiet, nearing 9PM, really quiet. Grindelwald was at the top end of the valley. No through automobile traffic. I paused, listened. Maybe I could hear the Lutschine River, about two hundred or so metres downhill, in the valley bottom. When I started walking again, all I could hear were my own footsteps.

Then somewhere up ahead, I heard what I instinctively knew had to be yodelling. Softly at first, then it filled my ears. It was like barbershop, a cappella, unaccompanied singing, a group. My ears carried me. My ears, transformed like a delicate cocoon, while the music wrapped me. I became suffused by an intense hypnotic, timeless, yet strangely joyful experience... softly I became... I was existing inside the music!

In no more than a hundred metres, and in the dark, the yodelling had led me just off the main street. On my left, behind a large tree, I saw a small shop or something, tucked behind a hillside. The yodelling was coming from that direction. On a softly lit, simple sign attached to the side of a smallish two story, free-standing building, I saw the name, Blumisalp Stubbe.

A Swiss stubbe is not like a British pub. Never in my time in Jungfrau Region Swiss stubbes did I see drunkenness or loutish behaviour—speaking of which, they are not for that same reason like American bars. The Swiss stubbes are community centres. They are additionally unique in that they often have long tables that accommodate many groups of people and individuals who share their stories of the day.

This Blumisalp stubbe had an outdoor terrace, facing the mountains, facing the Unterergletscher, and that was where I found the yodellers, about a dozen, maybe a dozen and a half of them. Everybody I knew always chuckled when yodelling was mentioned, something Americans had seen once back in the 1950s or early 1960s on the Ed Sullivan or the Lawrence Welk television variety shows.

But, in the still of these extraordinary evening mountains, in the quiet of the night, when the mountains were the foreground, middle ground and background, everything, that yodelling had a strong resonance that seemed at once appropriate to the scale of this place and respectful to its character.

I thought, I didn't know anything about this, so, who was I to judge... but... it did have a very nice feel, a certain sweetness, that's for sure. I stood and listened. I couldn't put words to it, but for the briefest moment, I thought I almost felt the very beginning of that same warm feeling of effulgences that had overwhelmed me in the cemetery. Then, as soon as the thought formed, the feeling was gone. The intimation disappeared, instantaneously absent. It was, nevertheless, in its brevity, enjoyable.

I stood inconspicuously on the edge of the stubbe terrace. All the stubbe terrace doors were open. The yodellers stood in two lines, at the side of the terrace, singing simultaneously to the mountains and the stubbe guests.

The yodellers were organized by height, shorter in front, taller in back. They yodelled two more songs that seemed to have verses and choruses, always a cappella. The singers were men and women, a combination of young and old. All in native clothes, somewhat Amish-like. Very clean costumes, dominated by black and white, well-pressed black trousers, white shirts and black vests with black lapels and black collars, tastefully accented with smallish embroidered wild flowers— gentian blues, edelweiss silver greens.

The men stood rather casually with their hands in their pockets, but there was definitely a grouped, a standing-in-lines organization. And the ladies, well, they, too, looked like Amish people, simultaneously proud and humble. Lots of white lace over black cloth, very discreet, no asset display. And the lace, very finely detailed, especially their headdresses, black caps with wide decorative white lace edges in a plant motif. They all looked like they were in their Sunday-go-to-church finest.

When the yodellers finished their number, an older gentleman, dressed the same way, set up what I knew to be from the hotel brochures an Alphorn. He performed one solo number that echoed back off the mountain faces. I was transfixed to the spot. When the Alphorn player had finished, there was a soft smattering of applause as he and the yodellers moved inside to sit down at one of the tables.

I finally moved my feet. That movement stirred my thoughts and broke me out of the music-induced daze. Music-induced daze? Ever before? Internal rolodex of memories whirred. Alhambra, Joaquin Rodrigo, Morocco, Umm Khaltoum— but this tonight was different. It was special. It had taken me through a new door.

I looked around. The stubbe was quietly busy, with two tables of customers out on the terrace. Inside, there were three very long tables with ten or more chairs each, and a bar with eight, maybe ten stools. The interior? Everything was hefty and made of wood, tables, chairs, walls and ceiling. Besides the yodellers, only ten or so other people inside, softly talking. No one paid attention to me.

The yodelling exuded the essence of all music... humans, without words, communicating from, and to, some magical landscape node. It was as if the jolly I had experienced in the Thunersee landscape the other day was the music I heard from the yodellers. How can I say this? Humans were the mouthpiece for the joyful energy in this landscape; and the yodel was the special music... a musical language of joy.

The yodelling had freedom, it had discipline, it had beauty and it conveyed, at the same time, a pleasant, almost jolly reverence, and an aura of relaxation.

I focussed on hearing, because it was hearing that enabled the yodelling to enter my being. Listening to music is a linear experience, just like walking through a garden, a landscape. Music and beauty. Gardens and beauty. Portals to transcendence. There had to be a linkage. Timeless experiences. Effulgences? Other worlds? I was back in the territory of the Oval and Obelisk gardens.

Magic in the landscape. Magic in the garden. That is allowed. That is its special character, its special quality. The magic must be there. Humans must find that magic and that, when found, turns mundane into... a proper garden, a proper landscape, a proper place for humans.

I almost had a grip on the essence of great design when I felt this magic in the yodeller music. I felt that same magic in the mountains yesterday. Magic two days in a row. Ruedi was right. He was not a travel agent. He had no financial "skin-in-the-game". I felt he had spoken from his heart. He had felt it and told me that I, too, should feel it. And I have.

This is the magic that must be an essential component in order to call "great" a designed garden or a designed landscape. I had been here before with my thoughts and dreams. They had been my hope from Tangier; but my years of practice in the "real world" had numbed those hopes.

Now they have been rekindled. But I still did not have a grip on useful vocabulary of that design. And more important, I had no idea how to design that magic into these human creations—the gardens, the landscapes.

I thought, this time I should explore this landscape further—as far as possible—there must be a secret for me to discover. These effulgences are too powerful to ignore.

✳✳✳

Kurt Says

I wanted more on design; and I got more. It's CJ and music. Here's how I understand it. People listen to music and get "in the groove". CJ imagines that people should be able to get "in the groove" when they walk through a garden or landscape. I can't immediately make that connection. CJ is trying. I am rooting for him. But, unfortunately, that may be CJ's design "utopia"—nice to have but unachievable in the real world.

I should note that in CJ's diary, he tied the yodelling experience to part of his strange garden experiences in Tangier. He also noted that the girl Bree whom he met in Casablanca also had heard unusual sounds in the North Africa landscape. He remarked that the sounds she heard were ugly and fearful while the Berner Oberland yodelling sounds he heard were beautiful. He described them as an effulgence. He wanted people to experience effulgences from his design.

He was out there. Far out!

And this place he visited was heavy. He found so many people deeply into that Berner Oberland landscape.

CJ had his fire on full. He was into it.

But as dreamy as his design writing was, I have to admit, I was intrigued. He was on his way... somewhere. He had hope. I had hope. My hope was selfish. I hoped he could explain that effulgent design in a way that I could apply it to my SoCal landscape architecture projects. Yeah, I had hope.

***

Suzanne de Sirmont

Inside the Blumisalp stubbe, I went up to the bar. The barkeep was female.

She approached me.

I said, "That yodelling... it entranced me. How is that possible? I've never heard anything like it. Does it have anything to do with the landscape? Who are these people?"

The barkeep looked me over, as barkeeps do, measured me without judgement in her eyes, and said, "Hello, they're from Grindelwald. They stop in about once a month. My name's Suzie, can I help you?"

"My name's CJ. I'm an American landscape architect—I worked the last six years in Saudi Arabia. I'm hungry and thirsty, what do you serve?"

She told me she made sandwiches and had a regional beer on tap.

I ordered a mountain cheese sandwich and a half litre Zwickel draft, the unfiltered beer I had enjoyed last night.

Suzie drew my draft beer and put it in front of me. She went back behind the bar, sliced the bread, buttered it, thin sliced the cheese and quartered a gherkin. After she made the sandwich, she plated it and delivered it to me.

I had already heartily drunk half my beer. As she served me the sandwich, she said, "Since you are a landscape person, I should tell you that this cheese and this beer are both local landscape products." I tucked into my sandwich and just watched the stubbe's activities slow down at the end of the night.

The yodellers had been sitting at one of the longer tables and having finished their small glasses of schnapps, were heading home. The rest of the tables gradually emptied and now, I had the barkeep more to myself—she had been welcoming—easy to talk with.

I started, "Suzie, I can't get that yodelling out of my head. And I mean that in a good way. I've often thought about music in the landscape and imagined individual landscape or garden rooms being similar to individual movements in a symphony... but after those yodellers, my music speculations seem so thin, so artificial... artificial impositions... actually struggles... but those yodellers tonight did something altogether different. Magic, they were magic! I don't know quite how to say this... as if the landscape itself was playing the tune through those yodellers... can that be... can you understand me? I can only call it magic."

Suzie listened, looked me in the eyes, and said, "*M'enfin*! You're really into it! I'll tell you what I've learned. Music experience is quite individual; but your words have a ring of truth. All those people are from families who have lived here many generations. This landscape is their life. And if there is magic in their music, that magic comes from the landscape."

"I don't know, I've tried to compare it to my past musical landscape experiences—an Egyptian singer, a Spanish composer—but this was so much... richer... fuller. Complete... in a transcendent sense."

She was quiet. I was quiet.

I finished my sandwich, and the rest of my draft. I had noted the landscape insight in her words and asked, "Are you, yourself, from Grindelwald?"

"*Moi? Je suis française*, born on Corsica; but I have lived here for nearly ten years now."

I looked at her. She was about thirty-five to forty, but even without makeup, looked like a well-kept late twenties. In her eyes, I saw the worldly knowledge of a barkeep, and a glimmer, a glimmer that hinted a deeper knowledge. I was not really sure what that glimmer was. But she had a trait, a characteristic that some French women display, a natural beauty of proportion and softness in her face that shows its best without noticeable makeup. And she spoke an English easy to understand.

I replied, "Corsica? That's amazing, how does a person from the wild isle of Corsica end up in Switzerland?"

She said with certainty, "You already know." I looked at her with uncertainty. She continued, "...mountains, landscape, the end of the road..."

"Yeah, I follow, Corsica and Grindelwald, both mountainous, both beautiful landscapes, both kind of end of the road, edge of civilization places... but why here? If I may ask, why did you leave your original mountain home?"

She explained that her parents had sent her to Grenoble for university. There she studied sociology, philosophy and minored in geology. But more so, she realized an exceptional attraction to the mountains. After graduation, she travelled and slowly worked her way through the French, Italian, Swiss, Slovenian, German and Austrian Alps. Then she did the same with the Pyrenees, from the Mediterranean to the Bay of Biscay. In the end, the Berner Oberland, the Jungfrau Region impelled her to stay.

She waved her arm outwards broadly to the mountains, then said, "The Jungfrau Region mesmerized me... just like you were entranced tonight by the yodellers, I was mesmerized by these mountains. By the way, do you know the history of the word mesmerize?"

"I know the word; but... tell me...."

"To hold the attention of someone to the exclusion of all else or so as to transfix them... well, more interestingly, it comes from a German physician, a guy by the name of Mesmer from the late 18th and early 19th centuries. He theorized that there was a natural energetic transference that occurred between all animate and inanimate objects. He spent his life trying to measure it, to prove it. The bottom line was he observed this strange force of attraction that still, even today cannot be measured. You were mesmerized by the yodellers, I am mesmerized by the mountains. We are both talking about some force... not defined by modern science. There is no metric for it. It is there, but no one can see it. A mystery it is."

"But you had mountains at home, no, and they had some attraction, didn't they?"

"I had a love of mountains at home since I can remember. When I went to university, I realized how great that love."

"What do you mean, 'love' of mountains? You say it with an emotional fullness that intrigues..."

"Mountains have character, CJ. I am not a person who conquers mountains, who climbs them and puts notches on my belt. I am a person who senses their character and shares. I open up to them. Some are threatening. Some are soothing. There are so many varieties; but these... these Jungfrau Region mountains... these inspire and comfort... and they are... simply... jolly!"

"Jolly? You said jolly?! I felt exactly that same way when I arrived here." I smiled as I spoke. We shared the smile and I continued, "So... you read the landscape, so to speak... or you hear the landscape... you share with the landscape... on an emotional level. Tell me more."

"While I was visiting all the Alps and Pyrenees, I went home from time to time to visit my parents and I found my attachment to mountains was greater than to Corsica. My great grandmother, I have taken her name, Suzanne de Sirmont. She came from a wealthy family, a titled family in Nancy. She gave it all up when she fell in love with a soldier, a farmer from Corsica. She left home, and powered by her love, followed him to Corsica. And three generations later, I, too, have that same strong love, but for mountains... so I, too, have left home to follow my love."

After the final customers paid up and left, Suzie went to clean up the last table.

***

Bruckner

Even though the landscape was my life's work, I had not really grasped my Swiss landscape experience yet. I recalled Ruedi's talk in Zurich about the special energy in this place, the Berner Oberland, the Jungfrau Region. Today, I had just met Ian and now this Suzie, both saying the same thing. And since my train ride in, two days ago, I hardly had a moment when I did not feel, in this place, some kind of extraordinary power, some kind of landscape power exerted on me.

Suzie paused next to me and said, "This landscape, these mountains... very powerful. CJ, let me put a CD on. There is music, a short motet written by Anton Bruckner, *Locus Iste*. Listen to it, many people hear it and say that it communicates the richness of presence they experience when they are in these mountains. Listen to it while I clean up, then tell me after what you think."

I listened. I thought, ...awe and reverence... yet... light-hearted... resonant but with a simplicity...

I said, "I'm having trouble trying to combine my experience at the church earlier today, with the yodelling, with my arrival experience yesterday and Bruckner's *Locus Iste*... it's not that they don't fit together, rather it seems that they demonstrate a richness of layers... which is parallel to the richness of presence I sense in these mountains... but there is definitely some kind of communication going on. But I do not know if I can say it is

102

love, as you do..."

"Some people get it, CJ, others don't... happens different ways to different people. Some people just walk right by as if there is nothing here!"

She continued cleaning up then returned to the bar. I said, "This afternoon, at the cemetery I saw a bushy haired, bushy bearded guy paying respects at a gravestone. I watched... wondered. Turned out he was a Scot, works in a bakery here, told me he'd been around here for years. Ian, yeah, Ian was his name."

"*Bien sur*, I know him. He's a hiker, not a climber, a hiker. He finds great places that others, besides locals, never find."

"Well, that's just what we're going to do the day after tomorrow... going to that glacier tongue right over there." I pointed across the narrow valley toward the Unterergletscher. "He called it the Malahide Walk. That's all he said. Not especially talkative... except on the subject of tourists."

Suzie had shut down most of the lights and came up to me and said, "Yeah, that's him, when it comes to tourists, don't get him started... but he has his own receptors to these mountains. He lives and breathes them. He thinks words get in the way more often than not. Sometimes, he just goes silent."

Then, for the briefest moment, as we looked each other in the eye, Suzie and I both went silent. The stubbe was already silent. That brief moment passed before emotions could overwhelm intelligence. Rather, I asked Suzie to play that Bruckner piece again. She put it on and prepared to lock up.

I felt strong emotion from the music and sensed a link with my processional entry to the mountains and lakes of the Jungfrau Region.

Bruckner's *Locus Iste* had a simplicity overlain with a richness in its flow. The more I listened to it, the more it seemed to have an aural flow like my visual ride into the Berner Oberland via the Thunersee.

Both seemed to have an underlying resonating base that had a life and complexity of its own. Both seemed to have a subtle, simple yet entrancing melody which had richness and intrigue woven within. They played back and forth across each other with a tension that challenged, that invited deeper inspection. Then when all came together in harmony, I lost track of time and place—that was the magic.

I wondered, if I can't verbalize it, how can I turn that experience into design, into a design protocol? I had been taken into other worlds. I had had worlds within worlds experiences. I struggled to fit these into my external vision, struggled to give them some design dimension that I could replicate. No success.

***

Algernon Blackwood

...in CJ's own words...

Suzie was just about ready to lock up when I asked her, "Have you heard of the Scot's Malahide Walk? Do you know anything about it?"

"I know the Malahide Walk. I know where it comes from. The Scot's a real Algernon Blackwood fan. Have you heard of Blackwood's short stories before?"

"Blackwood? No, tell me, I'm into books."

"Blackwood, Lovecraft... they are writers who, though called science fiction, are really writers who know how to exploit the subconscious or psychic links which most people, when they think about it, do really feel. Blackwood? He passed time in Switzerland where the forests mesmerized him; and he also went to Egypt. He was totally absorbed by forces in the landscape. Look, I have an old paperback of his. If you're interested, you can borrow it..."

"Definitely," I said. She went to a storage room behind the bar, came right back and handed the dog-eared paperback to me.

"Take a look at it. Look for the story, 'The Initiation'. That is where the Scot got his reference to a Malahide Walk. I'm told, Blackwood walked the Alps, not far from here."

I flipped through the book, looked at the table of contents and murmured as I read, "...Victim of Higher Space... interesting... The Willows... The Man whom the Trees Loved... plenty to read."

Suzie was ready to lock up.

"Take it with you if you like..."

"Sure, great... thanks."

We walked to the door together. She locked up and turned to go to her place—an apartment just up the outside stairs, above the stubbe storage rooms.

Suzie said, "Let's sit outside for a moment, under the stars, at the foot of these overwhelming mountains. Sit and listen to them with me."

We sat on a wooden bench against the wall of the stubbe. My head was in my hearing. It was quiet. Out of nowhere my yodelling experience linked to my hearing experiences in the Oval Garden decades ago. Hearing had to be the key. My question—key to which door where?

The mountain coolness started settling in on us, when Suzie said, "You spoke of an internal ecstasy in the presence of the mountains earlier. Carl Gustave Jung also wrote about that ecstasy and the human challenge of religious ecstasy, of transcendental ecstasy."

I listened.

"Jung wrote about a state of purest bliss, thronged round with images of all creation. Algernon Blackwood approached this same 'feeling' in some of his stories; but it was Jung who really got into it. Jung wrote visions of several images of 'mystical marriage'. Mystical marriage—a complex concept that has been expressed in the writings and artworks of alchemy, kabbala and some religions. The marriage occurs when two powers, such as the Chinese yin, the feminine, and yang, the masculine, are brought into harmony."

My thoughts were more on the mysteries of hearing and the importance of quiet. I said, "There are too many mysteries... too many ecstasies in these mountains. Too much everything. I am beat. I need to sleep."

I stood up. She stood up. I said, "I'll see you tomorrow but if not... for sure I'll stop by after I take the Malahide Walk with Ian. Thanks for the Blackwood book. I'm sure I'll get into it tomorrow."

I said goodnight and she kissed me on both cheeks. She was

106

a fine woman.

Again as I walked back to the hotel, the only sound... my footsteps. Sweet.

***

Vrnda Redux

...in CJ's own words...

As I began walking back to my hotel, I felt a chill in the air. Kept thinking about hearing as I walked. Suzie had said, listen to the mountains. The mountains paired with the quiet. Together, they released in me a glimpse of clarity.

At my hotel, blankets were provided for guests to sit in the garden patio chaise lounges. I thought of Hans Castorp in the *Magic Mountain* and his words "Take the cure that the mountain air offers". Inside, next to the doors to the garden, the blankets were folded and stacked. I took two blankets and went into the garden.

The chaise lounges were folded and stacked next to the building to keep them free of dew. I took a chaise lounge and set it up toward the southeast. I wanted only to listen.

I put one blanket over the lounge, sat, and stretched out my legs. Then covered myself with the second. I pulled it up over my shoulders and tight up to my neck. Then I tucked my arms under. I looked up at the mountains. Felt their brute strength. I warmed. My chill dissipated.

Now it was me, the mountain cliffs, their peaks, the cloudless sky and the quiet. Serenity. I breathed quietly. Relaxed. Thoughts began tumbling out. They flew.

I slept.

Blackbirds sweetly sang the praises of the approaching sunrise. I still slept. Until the sun peaked over the mountains.

And, with brightness and warmth, it shined on my face. I stood up, stretched and noticed the borrowed Blackwood book had fallen on the ground. I picked it up and I recalled that the last time I borrowed books... they were from Vrndadevi... I had not yet emailed her that they had been returned.

Back in my hotel room, I composed an email, thanking her for the books and the helpful discussions we'd had. I told her about the helpfulness of her friend. I let her know I had finished while in Geneva my quest for my friend.

I paused for a moment—Vrndadevi, Suzie, this landscape and music. I stepped over to my balcony, opened the door and stood before those mountains—those domineering mountains. Their strength, not for the first time, again gave me clarity. I wrote to Vrndadevi that I had followed her suggestions and in the footsteps of Mann and Hesse began exploring the Swiss Alp landscape, specifically the Berner Oberland, Jungfrau Region.

Vrndadevi's words about the material nature's modes of goodness, passion and ignorance kept bubbling up in my memory. Bubbling thoughts... with no tactile substance. I could not apply them to my experiences since I had arrived in the Jungfrau Region. Intense experiences. Everything had been so intense. I closed by thanking her for the books and the time we shared in the gardens of Ban Muang.

I sent the email, then got to thinking and writing. My time in the Swiss landscape, specifically the Berner Oberland Jungfrau Region, had been incredibly rich, fertile with design inspiration, fertile with people with whom I could talk and culturally share. This was about design. My experiences with plants and landscape—my design quest was being fuelled. Fuelled? Yes, but questions remained. I had rich experiences, true but the why and wherefore... elusive.

Plants, gardens, landscapes, I knew there was something healthy in that. Always something new to explore. And the musical aspect here was so prominent. On the train ride into this region what I saw caused me to sense music. Then there was the yodel and then there was Bruckner's *Locus Iste*. All these clues, newly placed in front of me.

As I mellowed in the recall of those recent feelings, my

memories of the Tangier Oval Garden times came back, piece by piece. I had once been convinced of the importance of hearing as a conduit to special realizations gleaned from plants and gardens. But I had lost all those realizations in my decades of professional practice.

I felt sad with those memories; but recharged to continue the hunt. There had to be something in the connection of hearing to my experienced landscape effulgences. Something measurable? Something arcane? I was eager to learn more.

My explorations and desired discoveries I hoped to share with other people. Why? It had to do with respect for landscape, gardens, plants... and respect for humans. Perhaps that hope was my motivation.

It was almost two in the afternoon. I shaved and prepared to go over to the Blumisalp Stubbe.

***

Uncle Alp

...in CJ's own words...

With music and landscape awhirl in my head, I had written intensely all morning. I finally took a break early afternoon and headed over to the stubbe. Suzie was there. She had been so very helpful in my design quest to understand this Berner Oberland landscape.

Suzie said, "*Ça marche bien?* How are you?"

"I'm good. What's up?"

"Do you have a little time?"

"Yeah..."

"Good, there's somebody here now who you should meet; but first, I want to do a little landscape experiment... are you up for it?"

"Yeah, tell me."

"I want to use the landscape to introduce you to somebody... so before I introduce you, step back out on the terrace and inhale the air... relish that fragrance, its depth of character, its breadth of satisfaction... really absorb it through all your senses, then come on back in."

I thought I'd go along with it, sounded interesting. I said okay. A bit bemused, I walked out on the terrace, now in full sun. I breathed in deeply. The sun's warmth and rays brought out the sweetness of the nearby pasture grass. I felt almost lightheaded... happy with a surfeit of energy in my lungs. I was smiling without inhibition when I went back inside.

Suzie smiled back at me. Handing me a couple thinnish,

bite-size slices of white cheese, she said, "Now try this cheese... savour it... tell me if it recalls any of what you have just experienced on the terrace."

The cheese was young, moist, yet firm. It did not give off a noticeable aroma. I took a bite. It was pleasantly mild at the front of my mouth. As I chewed it toward the back, I sensed what? An aroma? A taste with fragrance, like I was holding a huge armful of sweet, mountain pasture, wildflowers. I looked at Suzie. She was a teacher of the local landscape—never met anyone like her. My good fortune.

She said, "Now, let me take you over and introduce you to the local man who keeps the cows and makes that cheese, we call *muetschli*. He is a landscape man—a man born of these mountains. You might with benefit speak with him."

She walked me over to the far end of the bar, to an older farmer who, on my first look, reminded me of the upper Alpine grandfather character, Uncle Alp in *Heidi* as I had seen on one of the floors in the Zurich toy store, or maybe it was Peter Camenzind's father, I wasn't sure which.

Suzie introduced us to each other and helped us with language translation. Uncle Alp was not very talkative. He had his *krumme*, called cheroot, and his *stang*, his 300ml glass of beer.

Uncle Alp was a man of the era before the domination of skiing and hiking, before outsider recreation overtook local pasturage. He still had cows and goats and pasture to which he took them. He did it with the seriousness he had since his youth. But now it was different.

It was no longer about day-to-day mountain survival but rather survival of a centuries-old tradition of managing life and landscape in these mountains. He came to the stubbe this time of year as a midday break, almost as a social commitment.

When I met his eyes, I saw the history of the mountains, the peace of the mountain landscape. There was something absorbing about his eyes. They were the eyes of a person who had endured a huge amount of hardship, undergone huge amounts of austerity.

I recalled that once, Vrndadevi had quoted something

like, austerity is the wealth of the Brahmins. She had told me austerity develops a strength, gives a non-monetary wealth. His eyes were full of a mature tolerance born out of hardship, born out of austerity, eyes alive with a quiet and assured confidence that one often seeks from a best friend.

We shook hands, the rough hand of a lifelong farmer, named Peter, with the soft hand of a modern office person, mine.

But there was more; Peter's eyes, softly, but sharply, went directly to the back of my mind, that part that I usually protected, that part I usually kept to myself—my deep history, my motivations. Peter was in there, looked around, and left, before I could even think to blink my eyes or to turn my head. Peter's expression never changed.

Peter saw right through me. He saw my uncertainty, he saw the losses of my past, he saw the worn-out Band-Aid, my prideful design facade that covered my internal existential wound. His eyes required my humility, required I drop all pretence, all facade of being in charge of anything.

I was awash, I was at a loss. I was sitting in front of a man who had spent every day of his seventy or so years of life walking up and down these mountains, living within the grasp of these mountains. What could I ask? A numbing blank negated my mind, paralyzed my tongue. I had an able translator, what could I ask?

I finally said to Suzie, "Please ask Peter, what has he learned in these mountains that he must share with the youth of this area, with the tourists to this area?"

Suzie translated.

Peter never took the *krumme* out of his mouth. His expression did not change. He sat silent. He looked out at the midafternoon mountains. His *krumme* gave off slight swirls of soft smoke. Still, he sat silent. Then, taking the *krumme* out of his mouth, he said, "The *alp* gives life. The *berg* takes life. Protect the *alp*. Fear the *berg*." He drew deeply on the *krumme*. Slowly he exhaled... looked at me, then Suzie, before he took a long pull from his *stang*. Then his eyes went back to the midafternoon mountains, the *berg*.

113

I later learned that an *alp* was a botanically rich pasture grassland and the *berg* was the above-the-tree-line-stone-faced mountain. But in the moment, I had few intelligent thoughts.

I asked Suzie, "What does he mean?"

Suzie answered, "Peter's heart, his entire life is in these mountains. He is not a romantic. He is a realist. Life is hard here. Life is lost... weather, topography, geology, all undermine even the most intelligent, determined and heartfelt plans and actions of the people who live here. But the *alp*, the productive fields, pastures and forests, they give life, a life to be proud of, a life of simplicity, a small footprint, a life full of joy, daily hard work, and material satisfactions, but not in the excesses of modern culture."

I thought Peter spoke in aphorisms, like Ruedi's riddles; so I asked Suzie, "I guess I understand it as a statement about life in these mountains? The mountains teach that there is never true freedom from the struggle for existence. The mountains, through plants, soil, water give us a satisfying way to live... but they are also dangerous... is he saying that?"

"I think that's a fair summary." Then she added, "Let me tell you a little more about him, it will help you understand... he comes in all the time... like Ian, he doesn't speak much, but he does not have that wild anger that Ian has. Peter has an easy helpfulness and understanding in his manner. He, too, feels the special energy here. But the old timers never talk about it to foreigners, to tourists, to strangers... they carry it with them, in their hearts. They protect it, they nurture it... an oral tradition, no, a spiritual tradition, something both spiritual and, at the same time, greater than religion. The best of the yodellers exude it. In fact, those yodellers last night... one was his niece, another his nephew and the young boy was his grandson."

Peter stood up and asked, "Anything else?"

He put four francs on the bar and started out the door, saying, "*Adieu, wiede leuge.*" I was silent. Suzie smiled and said goodbye to Peter, "*Schoene.*"

"That's the best picture of a man and the landscape you will ever find," she said. Then, looking me in the eyes, she

114

continued, "People protect this mysterious good they have here. They know how easy it is to lose it, to lose their life in this place where from time to time the forces of nature remind humans how weak and how insignificant humans are. Peter realizes that and is, thus, innately humble."

I wondered about his demure presence and my passionate seeking. The difference? Age? The alps? Was I misdirected? Was design, as Gordie and Ruedi had suggested—just a flimsy social construct? Because here there was beauty in the landscape... and no landscape architect.

Suzie could see me in thought. She paused before continuing, "Hubris, and its lesser cousin, pride, need to be kept in check. Humility is important; but just being humble does not make the balance work. Pride, as a human drive, is a two-edged sword. Becomes hubris. The drive needs to be controlled, directed for good, not for greed, not for excessive desire for honour. Mountain people, like Peter, know how to keep hubris and pride in their place. They understand the importance of self-control and discipline. They live it."

I heard Suzie well. A lifetime in this landscape requires humility and practicality. I imagined that as Uncle Alp walked up toward Bort from the stubbe, he heard the birds, he felt the wind, he saw the clouds, he thought there comes a time in life, after so many decades, after so much has changed, when it is clear that death cannot be far...

***

Gnomes

...in CJ's own words...

Uncle Alp's presence had stirred unusual thoughts for me. Thoughts that undid my premise of design importance.

I worked in a profession where humility might lose me work. Landscape architects were always in battles with architects, engineers and planners—who should do what. We called those battles—turf wars.

I felt the need to lighten up—in my own way. I changed the subject from humility and hubris, speculating with a smile, "I should have asked Peter about gnomes..."

Suzie laughed and said, "You've got to be kidding. You want gnomes, then go to the Coop, the local grocery and home goods store, they sell them for decorating your garden. You call them gnomes; here, we call them *zwergs*."

I said, "Myself, I've never got past Snow White and the Seven Dwarfs. But as my train departed from Interlaken, the other day, I did notice, here and there, around chalet front doors and gardens, little thirty-centimetre-tall gnomish-looking dwarfs. There were too many and too much variety in shape and age. It couldn't have been fashion, could it? So, I was figuring there was something in the local legends, in their tales, in their sagas..."

"Listen CJ, the gnomes, locals call them *zwergs*, their stories were here before the tourists... so, what could I say? I suppose... I could say myth. Or, no myth. What is the difference? It is all real... gnomes." Suzie looked out the window at the Shreckhorn, then said, "Gnomes... I'd say, they fit comfortably into a chiaroscuro, if you know the word?"

"Yeah, yeah, I know it."

"Well, gnomes are... a chiaroscuro between history and reality. But, I can say that I myself have never seen..." She was still smiling when she continued, "Maybe I haven't been here long enough, yet. Nobody's let me in on it... say, I see some new people just came in at the long table by the door... be right back."

Much later, I did some digging into gnomes and their legends. I realized that the chiaroscuro Suzie spoke of was the very same chiaroscuro found in every culture where the edge of written history meets the edge of spoken history.

Enlarge the magnification on your look at where those two edges of history meet and there you have chiaroscuro, a fog of uncertainty... in other words... gnomes and the landscape... your guess is as good as mine.

Chiaroscuro had a nice artistic pencil or charcoal sketch meaning for me. But it also held the unknown, the existential mysteries of humans. Maybe I could call it the "twilight zone".

When I explored the landscape I was not looking for existential clues, I was looking for design roots. That the clues and roots may be one and the same never occurred to me.

In the Berner Oberland I became mystified by music and its unusual combination of jolly and reverence in the landscape. Though I was examining many threads in the landscape cloth, that jolly, reverential music and landscape was a new thread gaining strength, a thread meriting deeper exploration.

***

Rory McGuffin

...in CJ's own words...

My thoughts drifted. Suzie was busy with customers. I was just about ready to go back to the hotel to do some writing when she stopped by and said, "See that guy over there at the long table on the left, at the end, by the window? He's an American, been working here for two years now as a dishwasher, in the downstairs cook's kitchen at a hotel, just down the street. Might be fun to talk with him..."

"Thanks, Suzie."

I finished my beer, went over to the long table and sat down across from the guy Suzie had pointed out. "Hi, my name's CJ, I'm an American, a landscape architect... Suzie told me you're American and working here, is that right?"

With gusto and a big smile, the dishwasher reached out to shake my hand, saying, "Hi, my name's Rory, Rory McGuffin. Yeah, I'm American. And you, you're a landscape architect? You're kidding! Me, too!"

I said, "Two American landscape architects?! Hey, let me buy you a beer—we'll toast the profession. I studied at Michigan State, where are you from?"

"Another Midwesterner! Me, I'm from Chicago but not exactly, I'm from a south suburb, Calumet City. You've heard of Cal City, haven't you... Blues Brothers?"

"Who hasn't? Blues Brothers—Belushi, Ackroyd, the Chicago police... some real craziness..." I laughed and was still laughing when he joked, "Yeah, but tell me, Rory, how does a Cal City criminal become a landscape architect?" Laughing ourselves silly, we Midwesterners toasted our profession and chugged our first beer in competition. Rory finished first. I bought the second round.

"So tell me, Rory, about your school and how you ended up here, what, washing dishes?"

"Environmental Science undergrad, MLA, University of Illinois, that's the story, long and sweet."

I looked him over as he spoke. Rory, obviously a recent graduate, had a nervous tic of some kind. He could not look me in the eye without a quick flick away of his own eyes and head. His hair was in a men's pageboy with long bangs. Each time his head flicked, his hair fell in his eyes and then Rory struggled again to flick his hair back out of his eyes. And then, the hair would immediately fall back into his eyes again. Very hard to listen with so much head and hair movement, so much visual distraction. I observed a fine, but feckless, fitfully flapping youth. That was the book cover.

In the background, the stubbe sound system was playing the Berner Oberland radio station, an unusually eclectic mix, in a way not too different from elevator music. "Beds Are Burning" was on, by the Australian group, Midnight Oil. Rory was tapping out the beat with his fingers on the table, rocking his head. Rory sang along—something about giving land back to the Aborigines. Touched a nerve, it did in me.

Neo-romantic environmentalists, I thought. They are ignorant of the real history of humans and the landscape. These days they don't teach as they did before—a reality succinctly summarized by Hesse's observations in Peter Camenzind, where he described life of humans and the landscape: "the wretchedness of a life of unrelieved toil and dependence on the forces of nature"—that was man and the landscape!

I was tempted to stereotype Rory. Eco-wacko. Undergrad in Environmental Science. Then he took one of those one-size-fits-all three-year Masters of Landscape Architecture. Professional degree program, they call it. What that really meant was that Rory did not know much about landscape architecture, probably just wanted nature to be untouched,

119

maybe "restored" to some stilted, politically correct, arbitrarily static past condition—unless, of course, it got in the way of his personal life. I snickered to myself... youth, the Eleusinian feast, but...

I offered a friendly challenge. "Have you traded landscape architecture for the life of a ski bum?"

"To tell you the truth... I hadn't really thought about it... but, hey... why not? I'm having too good a time here in Grindelwald, a simple sustainable lifestyle—skiing, working, playing! I'm not giving that up. But what about you—what are you doing—you working or what?"

I chewed on it for a minute. Gave a straight answer. "I've made my commitment to professional landscape architecture. I work in international development. I like the challenges; but it has its downsides... slowdowns... I'm between projects right now."

"Why, hell, between projects? Can there be a better place to come and chill? Don't you like this landscape?"

"Yeah, I do, no question."

"Keep it simple, like me, CJ. I just might be a ski bum because, you know how a surfer lives every day to be on those waves... I, like, live that way for fresh powder snow, the blue sky, the cold air in my face! There's a buzz in all that! And what can I say—the party scene afterwards, the wood fires, the girls... oh yeah, I like the landscape here!"

As soon as he finished his pitch to me, Rory turned his attention to the two girls who had just sat down across from him.

I thought, even though my profession is busy placing plants around humans, my profession is derelict in its duty to humans and plants because it does not address any life cycle issues in plants or humans. And Vrndadevi talked about all life forms as having the spark of God in them, thus needing to have human custodianship. That makes sense in the obvious order of life on the planet. Humans as stewards! Old memories returned... wasn't that what those Tangier botanists said was the essential first step in working with plants—a stewardship attitude?

I was caught up in those thoughts, then wondered if there

might ever be an episode in Rory's life that would enable him, chasten him to gain the steel and discipline I had met earlier in Uncle Alp. Maybe Rory was one of those hope-I-die-before-I-get-old types. Maybe he was part of that newest generation that thought the "struggle for existence" was nothing more than a conservative old-folks meme of "days gone by".

Enough was enough! I drained my *stang*, stood up, shook hands with Rory, wished him the best, and said good night.

I needed to hit the rack early because of my 5AM hike the next morning. I went to the bar, found Suzie, thanked her for all the introductions to locals, said goodnight, then walked back to my hotel.

Along the way I remembered I had the Algernon Blackwood short story, *The Initiation* to read. Suzy had recommended it. She said Ian took the name Malahide Walk from it.

Before I went up to my room, I stopped at the hotel desk to make sure I would get a wakeup call at 4AM. The desk clerk gave me a message that had been left by Ian. The Scot confirmed he had socks and hiking shoes for me. He also wrote he would bring some eatables and drinkables for us both, reminding me he would be seeing me at 5AM tomorrow in front of the Ringgenberg Bakery.

I went up to my room, sat down for a moment and did some writing—meeting Rory had got me thinking about my profession back in the US. I had been looking for weak cracks in contemporary professional and cultural facade where ancient roots might break through. I was hunting for clues when I wrote that these days, the oracles of landscape architecture talk a lot about design. But that talk is a shabby cover. It is sophistry with a thin frosting over a cake made by scientific analysis and conscripted regulatory requirements.

Landscape architecture jobs come into the professional office for design and go out to construction with nary a thought about the life cycle of the plants involved—their growth, old age, disease and death. Those holistic issues were a big part of alchemy and once again were touched briefly in the advancing thinking of the Age of Reason.

As the results of mechanization brought an industrial age,

these same items were recalled by the Romanticists. But now, after the industrial age and now the information age, in my profession, in academia, in practice, nobody talks about them.

Plants have become plant materials—something an Italian Futurist would have been proud of.

Strangely, superficial sustainability has become a worshippable secular god! No definitions... the blindness of being lost in a fog. That is the worshippable secular god of the green modernity!

It all seems so backwards or blind these days. So this pop-sustainability... I find it strange—but maybe standard for a contemporary world that is consumed with pop-everything. Clever is better. Superficial is good—incredible—blind in a white-out fog is good?!! No!

Pop stuff and pop landscape architecture is about things. Things! Not life, not life forms, not life cycles.

As if it is not important to understand the broad range of qualities that plants bring to their service of humans—as if humans had no responsibility, no stewardship.

As if all the "improvements" made through industry, technology and information need not be applied to the lives of plants?!

Ignorance.

Those gross and subtle advancements must have their place in design. Stewardship has to be integrated with design. Otherwise, design is itself just a piece of plastic furniture! Here today, gone tomorrow! ...whisps in the fog...

As much as Rory's self-interested hedonism under the jargon of sustainability bothers me, it does signify an important fundamental. Regardless of their jargon and branding, people like Rory recognize that the landscape is important. And that it should be part of their lives. That is good. That is a start.

I stood up and stretched. I saw the Blackwood book on my dresser. Yeah, I was done writing for the night. Took a shower, got ready for bed and began to look through the Algernon Blackwood collection of short stories. I read the shortest ones first. When it came to landscapes and plants, Blackwood knew how to write. His writing carried my mind to landscape places previously inaccessible.

Then I got into *The Initiation*. Blackwood's story took me on a walk through the Alpine forests that I myself would soon be seeing. The story told of a visitor to the Alps who was casually walking through the evergreen forest. The silence, the light beams deep in a dense, shady evergreen coniferous forest slowly transformed into a palpable, a visceral energy, a force that the visitor totally absorbed—time and space melted away.

I wondered if my hike tomorrow in the forests would enchant like Blackwood. Would some kind of force or presence overwhelm my normal experience of time and space? Ruedi said so. Ian said so. But I was only hopeful, not convinced. Would it be similar to, or an expansion of what I felt in the cemetery yesterday? In these thoughts, I drifted off to sleep. I slept peacefully. I slept well.

***

Malahide Walk

...in CJ's own words...

T he phone rang. The wakeup call. It was 4AM. Time to get up. I couldn't even remember falling asleep. I pushed myself up, got ready. Headed for the Ringgenberg Bakery, my 5AM rendezvous with the Scot.

The Scot had for me boots, heavy socks, a rucksack and provisions for our five-to-six-hour hike. We sorted who would carry what, and took off. The pre-sunrise sky was already light when we started off downhill toward Grund, our lowest elevation, just under 1,000 metres above sea level, then up gradually along the Lutschine River with its thickets of alders, then back uphill in the direction of first the Gletscherschlucht, then the Unterergletscher. We entered a mixed forest of Norway spruce, maples and maybe a beech clump or two, at the base of the Eiger, and pushed upward, past a sign that warned all not to proceed due to danger of falling rocks.

Through the mixed forest, climbing steadily upward, approaching fifteen hundred metres elevation, we walked along the base of a cliff. The deciduous trees gradually disappeared as we climbed higher. The forest became denser with Norway spruce, coniferous trees well over 100 feet tall.

We paused for a brief rest. Ian asked about the landscape of the Arabian desert. I explained, "Unlike the plant rich 'deserts' in the Southwest US, there were huge expanses of sand deserts on the Arabian Peninsula, without plants... no plants at all!

"The desert was extremely straightforward, extremely

124

unfriendly to humans. It was very black and white there, very either-or. Either there was water or there was not water. The most dominant realization was... lack of water meant lack of life." I paused.

Ian asked, "Without water, are there any humans?"

"Humans... there are the Bedouins. They move with the rainfall. They travel oasis to oasis. They are like the grasses that appear only after a rainfall. And disappear sometimes for years. Bedouins are landscape people. Live a hard but simple nomadic life. Pleasure from making their own stories, their own music—hand-clapping and lute. But... always, always chasing for water." I paused again.

Then continued, "To imagine a surfeit of water, topsoil, green plants like we see here all around us, this incredible richesse... that would be well beyond a mirage... well beyond the wildest dream."

Ian nodded, showed that he understood.

As we looked back into the large, broad bowl of rich agriculture below us in the Grindelwald Valley, Ian and I stood speechless. We saw its full breadth, stretching from our feet down to Grund. It was a huge bowl, rolling back up to the Dorf, then higher still up to the two thousand metre First. Then finally to the twenty-nine-hundred-metre peak where the first warming sun rays softly kissed the Schwartzhorn then the Faulhorn. We watched the sun sweep over all of the peaks and ridges stretching to Grosse Scheidegg.

Sunrise in the Jungfrau Region. The beauty was magnificent. It was massive—like taking in the deepest breath of fresh air—energizing.

I finally said, "Ian, you said you were from the Isle of Skye. Like most people I've heard of the Isle of Skye and its natural beauty—does it compare to what's in front of us right now?"

"Not really," he started, then, "...well, yes and no."

"Tell me about it."

"Before us in the Grindelwald Valley, we see a lot of the signs of human habitation over the surface of a spectacular landscape. On the Isle of Skye, especially my favourite area the Black Cuillin, there is nary a sign of humans. The landscape is rugged, a bit like here... I remember seeing a print in your hotel one time, something by Turner, called Lake of Thun. In his depiction of water, light and mountains I saw landscape character like the Black Cuillin, especially around Lake Coruisk, where I always hiked.

"Both have stunning landscapes that overwhelm me. But the Black Cuillin landscape is stern, it's wild... it's dark... here, the landscape is accessible and accepting on so many levels... it heals... it soothes. I don't want to be romantic about it; but that's how it works on me."

Ian stopped talking, started walking. I followed. We continued upward through the spruce forest on a path that would certainly take us out of the Grindelwald Valley.

We followed the rising terrain and then over a crest, still in deep spruce forest. We continued on an old, but not well-worn path as the terrain fell away under the forest canopy. Finally, up ahead, a view emerged, a view up to a hulking, huge glacier, high on a steep slope. Though the glacier was probably a good four kilometres away, I could still see the seracs, pointed out by Ian, the individual, vertical ice tongues, at its front edge.

Ian noticed that I was stunned by the view. He offered, "You're looking at what remains of the Unterergletscher, the lower Grindelwald Glacier, where it connects to the Unters Ischmeer, the lower Ice Sea. I recall also in your hotel a print of work from the 1830s by an artist, Fearnley, Thomas Fearnley, showing those seracs right down into the Grindelwald Valley at the edge of Grund—10 kilometres from where it is today!"

Having seen other art depicting the glacier from just over a century ago, I could not believe how far the glacier had receded, and remarked so to Ian.

Ian said, "That glacier is alive... it breathes... on a different time scale... it has always been growing and receding. Before the recent Little Ice Age, which began about 600 years ago, these glaciers had receded a whole lot more than what you see now. They're always active."

We walked on to a larger clearing at the edge of the forest, with an Alpine meadow at our feet. We had been hiking for three hours. We sat down on a boulder, near the edge of a rock scree.

Ian pointed upward and out to the left to the Mettenberg mountain, well above the tree line, where if we were lucky we might see Alpine Ibex, Steinbocks, foraging the nearly barren, rocky slopes. He swept his arm along the panorama and commented on all the varied size streams of snow melt; each and every rivulet had action, all collecting beneath them in the huge moraine, left by the receded glacier, all collecting into the Schwarze Lutschine, the Black Lutschine River flowing through the Gletscherschluct.

We had arrived in an unusual place. Around us... the silence of no human mechanical devices. The mountain topography had separated us from all reference to human activities in the Grindelwald Valley. Was this Ruedi's energy source? Yet I wondered, what was I hearing? Did I have tinnitus? No, that must have been the Lutschine and all its collecting rivulets, draining the glacier, creating white noise.

I longed to be free from that noise, that noise that I often thought was the same as the running noise generated by many cars on a West LA freeway, the same noise as the non-stop AC in Saudi. White noise, boon or curse? Maybe my hearing was not sensitive enough to distinguish between the mechanical white noise of human devise and the natural white noise of the ice-melt rivulets. After all, I was surrounded by the fullness of springtime weeping from the high Alpine landscape, powered by gravity.

I shared those thoughts with Ian, and the Scot replied, "Listen carefully to the sound of that water... it changes throughout the hour, throughout the day... it changes every day... it changes with the weather... with the seasons. Think of it as the language of the mountains... some call it the songs of the mountains. Each rivulet has its own character, its own sound."

We opened our rucksacks and took out the snacks. We ate some *schnarken*, hazelnut-paste-filled sweet rolls, and drank Rivella, a carbonated, sweetened whey drink. Those refreshed and tasted nice; but I was still bothered by my hearing. The noise of chewing and drinking was exaggerated, almost splitting in my ears. I couldn't believe that I might actually be missing 21st century urban background noise. But, after the Scot's explanation of the songs of the mountains, I focussed on the water flow in the nearby rivulet, and it did calm me.

We sat in the sun. After a while, I said, "You know, after my hearing settled in and after my mind absorbed the character of the sounds up here, I've started to think differently... there is a so-called 'quietness' up here; but it is weird... something about it stretches logic or invalidates common sense... it's beyond me... maybe a bit like what some in other circumstances have identified as a literary high... there is something simultaneously abnormal and attractive about it."

Ian asked, "What do you mean?"

"Normal reality's not fully comfortable, there's always some kind of uneasiness in our normal lives. And this experience up here, I've come to feel, is more comfortable, ergo, more natural? This experience reveals something that is normally covered. That's the uncomfortable part. So, what do we do, chase after the natural, chase after the natural high? So what, then you find it; but how, how practical is it to live 24/7/365 here? You know... thirst, hunger and the need to eliminate..." I trailed off, unconsciously losing ground on some kind of dead-end logic.

"On the other hand," Ian offered, "if this experience is like a battery recharge, then just like re-chargeable batteries, the recharging is not optional, it is a must."

I nodded agreement.

We sat quietly in the sun, finishing our snack. Ian pointed to the butterflies passing by now and then—Adonis Blue, Marbled White. He had both knowledge and feeling for this landscape, and its components.

In the quiet I thought about nature, the landscape, design and my experiences. I looked at the glacial mountain streams above the treeline—clear and white, straight flow to the pineal. Words and talking get in the way. The streams continue but when talking begins, the pineal flow stops. I could say that the streams take advantage of the eyes and ears as paths to the pineal.

128

And views? What about views? What is it that is the view? It is an energy source seeking the pineal. Don't turn away until you feel it. My thoughts were flowing freely. What my senses were absorbing was too varied and too intense to let my design speculations enter.

Then Ian said, "We talked about art earlier. Art is really just a cheap surrogate. What we see in front of us is the real thing. This is the re-charge. And the sad thing... there is a sad thing... I use the Google Earth software and the numbers of geo-referenced photos for this area have geometrically increased the last couple years... like an electronic human extension reaching up from the Grindelwald Valley."

Then Ian launched, "This is why more and more tourists bothers me. Too many of them bring so much of the wrong kinds of energy. They are net drainers or net coverers of the positive energy in this landscape. They treat this landscape at best like an old-fashioned zoo, walking around haughtily as if they own the whole frickin' thing.

"They are an imperialist curse... their presence here... their kind of landscape tourism. Who is the imperialist? They are! They come like they are entitled to it, bad behaviour and all. Who can afford to visit as a tourist? Who can be away from his work and not jeopardize his life, his livelihood?

"Who can come to have his picture taken in front of a mountain... come to have his picture taken next to the Alp farmer, next to the alphorn player, next to the yodeller, or, for that matter, in your sand desert next to the Bedouin, next to the lute player... then go back home and back to work? Do they give anything in return? I could care less about carbon calculations; but noisy busses, crowded trains, bolshy private cars, and bolshy, selfish tourists, they suck the heart out of the landscape. I ask again who is the imperialist? It's the nouveau riche, middle class, upper class! This place is so much more than a number on someone's bucket list!"

As we looked out and up in the direction of the edge of the upper Ice Sea, its power softened the conversation, changed its focus.

Ian pointed up toward the tops. "Up there, that is just

the beginning of the Aletsch Glacier... it travels south, continuously for more than 15 kilometres with many branches, and dominates more than one hundred square kilometres, some places as thick as a thousand metres... always influencing the human culture along its edges. That glacier links cantons, Wallis and Bern, and its landscape plays a huge historical role, if that's what interests you."

Ian continued, "In the old days, before the Little Ice Age, Berner people used to bring their alphorns here, as did the people from the Walliser, the Valais side. They would play back and forth to each other across this valley, now filled with the Aletsch Glacier. We'll have to be satisfied with this view today. To explore further will be a walk for another day." We gathered our things, put on our rucksacks and headed back down to Grindelwald.

***

Malahide Decompression

...in CJ's own words...

Arriving back in Grindelwald, we were talking as we entered the stubbe for a beer. Suzie came up to us and asked, "How did it go?"

"The Scot got me up close to the edge of the glacier, Suzie. It was spectacular! I had no idea that before the Little Ice Age it was hikeable. He told me about how they communicated with alphorns... communicated... not just musical performance."

I paused, then continued, "But I'll tell you. Thanks to the Scot, I'm beat. I'm not used to exercise like this."

Ian laughed as he got up to leave. He shook hands with me, and I, with a smile, said, "Ian, that was great fun. Thanks for setting me up with the kit and all the conversation. Maybe we can do this again sometime, maybe a full day and go all the way to the glacier itself, eh? ... and, to make the longer distance, I'll need my own hiking boots for sure."

Ian smiled and said, "Let's do that, but not for the next couple weeks. Will you still be here?"

"Good question. We'll see."

Before Ian left the stubbe, he reminded me to pick up my shoes at Ringgenberg's.

Then Suzie said, "You thanked him for the conversation? That guy is almost as taciturn as Uncle Alp!"

I said, "He introduced me to the life and history of the edge of the glacier up there. He revealed a bit of what makes him tick. You were right, he is another person magnetized by this

131

landscape. But he did flash again on the increasing tourists... and I'll tell you, I was surprised to feel a bit myself of what he was talking about... if I was not a committed professional landscape architect..."

A couple customers came in and took Suzie away.

She returned as I drained my *stang*. "Give me another, please."

Suzie served me another and told me her help had arrived so she had some time right now. She asked what else had I seen up on the hike today... any Steinbocks or other animals?

I told her about the butterflies. "I never expected butterflies on the edge of the glaciers... such a lightness against those massive stellacs... and the huge scale of those mountain peaks and ice seas! There is so much..."

"You like butterflies? There is a place I like to hike where the shade is very cool and in the sun it's very warm, soothing... it is out of the way and I go there just to let the sun energize my skin... it's kind of a naturalist way of quiet enjoyment... lots of butterflies dancing everywhere. If that interests you, I can take you there on my day off if the weather is good."

"That would be nice. When?"

Just then her help called her and she was off, leaving me to muse and linger over my *stang*. I finished my beer before Suzie was free again. As I started to leave, I passed by Suzie and asked, "Hey Suzie, you on duty tonight?"

"*Bien sur*, I have my Lauterbrunnen friend coming over later this evening. From a family living here many, many generations—actually the story is that her family originally migrated from across the way, from Valais—because over there, the rainfall was so low and the soil so thin. That is how you get French sounding names in this German speaking area. She is young, educated and really has a unique perspective on the local landscape... deep ecologist... so make sure to come back this evening, ok?"

"Definitely, see you later."

***

Kurt Says

CJ was on the hunt to learn as much as he could about this Swiss mountain landscape. He was a man on a mission. He had strength and commitment.

His attraction to the gothic fairytales of Algernon Blackwood told me I was right. CJ's design quest was one step beyond. CJ's design ideas were "Twilight Zone" material. But they were intriguing.

Judge for yourself.

***

Mazy Design Skeins

...in CJ's own words...

After returning to my hotel room, I went out onto my terrace. The view was astounding, unbelievably large, expansive. I could hardly take in the massive mountains in my face, the Shreckhorn, the Eiger and between them the dramatic gorge, the Unterergletscherschlucht.

I looked for the areas that I had, for six hours, walked through, with my memory and eyes retracing my paths. I had been in the same area that Ruedi, in Zurich, had recommended and identified as an energy source.

I recalled how I had been invigorated up there at the foot of the massive Lower Ice Sea and its lower Grindelwald glacier—after I had climbed out of the Grindelwald Valley—after I became accustomed to that strangely quiet but noisy space. I recalled how the noise transformed into music. I was inspired.

The landscape is the source of my design inspiration. When I feel the inspiration like I did up there, all issues material—thinking, feeling, willing—dissipate... even disappear. I reflected—the Berner Oberland landscape had rekindled every dream I had about transcendent experiences in the landscape—if writers, composers, musicians could get there, why not landscape architects?

Landscape is my path to plants, gardens, design. My goal is to find a way to share that special "music" I experience with other humans who will journey through my projects.

When I was working, doing my professional landscape

architecture activities, there was never any discussion of spiritual relationships between humans and the landscape. But my discussions, with Vrndadevi at Ban Muang, and then with Ruedi, Suzie and the others here, were dominated by spiritual relationships between humans and the landscape.

At the feet of these majestic Jungfrau Region mountains, in these last days, looming larger than anything, was my memory of the train ride into these mountains. It was about design. On that ride, I had been absorbed with what I had experienced in the Berner Oberland landscape—a dynamic sequence of unique spaces.

In each of those spaces had been intense, densely packed experiences one after another—ecstatic landscape experiences.

But on top of that was the most resonant landscape memory... yodelling. It was, for me, the first time landscape and music truly mated. That yodeller group in Grindelwald... it was magic. That music took me on a magical journey... a ride like I had never experienced.

I concluded one similarity between experience of listening to music and experience of moving through the landscape. They both were linear.

I tried to break down, to understand in detail these two separate linear movements. Both took me on journeys through windows to transcendent beauties. Both movements took me to a special place. Both included indescribable effulgences replacing my consciousness of senses, mind and intelligence.

The yodeller music linear experience was outdoors, at night, in the face of the mountains. It lasted fifteen minutes and entered through my ears.

My other linear experience was my spectacular entry procession movement through the Jungfrau Region landscape. This entered primarily through my eyes over a period of hours in three stages, on the train, on foot and while I sat on a bench.

It began on the Thunersee and culminated on that Grindelwald bench, where I was "possessed by the mountain landscape".

I struggled to tease out some kind of design protocol from these landscape and music experiences.

Design Protocol 1.00

Distant view, then procession, then detail inspection of the components of the original distant view. That is the core thread, the core structure, the core linear sequence of any garden or landscape experience. Without that sequential thread, it is impossible to find the window for the emergence of transcendent beauties.

In views and procession, there must be control of light and control of vision. Without those controls the emergence of transcendent beauties cannot occur.

Corollary 1.01

My experiences in Tangier, Ban Muang, and the Jungfrau Region all had something in common—something essential according to Tolly and Fyodor—stewardship. Vrndadevi called it service. And here in the Berner Oberland farmer stewardship of the landscape was obvious. People had been living here for the better part of a millennium and they still had a landscape of redoubtable beauty. This corollary is one word—stewardship. In it is embodied a love of the landscape—a love of service. Without that, no design will succeed. Maintenance, which some might say is synonymous, is a 10-cent word that does not have love or service or stewardship implied.

Design Protocol 2.00

Not ready yet. Something about hearing, music and how those can weave together threads of spirituality, design and landscape.

Here is where I entered the clouds of uncertainty. Hearing... the music... I'm just not sure of that linkage. The landscape here has inspired composers, authors, artists.

I hear the music, it takes me on a ride. I see the landscape and the train takes me on a ride. Can the two fit together? What are the connectors? And what about the ride I take walking along a path through a garden?

And the yodelling... that was different altogether. It was mystical. I did not know what that was all about... but it took some power from the landscape and wrapped me in it. My ears were essential. Other people were essential. Mystical...

magical... controllable? Could it be extracted and repeated in landscapes and gardens? In places other than right here in the Berner Oberland, the Jungfrau Region?

My design quest into landscape, gardens, plants, music—in those I have drive—I have strength.

I dug into it some more—both music and landscape mesmerized me—and here in the Berner Oberland Jungfrau Region they came together. Was it as simple as kismet, as coincidence? Or had I stumbled through a door into another dimension for landscape architecture design?

I had trouble with generating enough logic, even the proper vocabulary to generate a draft design protocol. I concluded that I must still be missing some important pieces. There must be some arcane threads that if found would make clear my design direction.

I seemed about to conclude on a vocabulary. I was thinking metaphorically about threads that could be weaved, woven and wrapped into skeins. These special skeins included plant threads. Then the skeins could transport humans into the experience of transcendent beauties. Without the plants, the skein could not be woven.

I asked myself, how does the thread get woven and wrapped into skeins? And how do the threads come about?

I speculated that the threads from plants in gardens and landscapes might be vitalized mentally by human intent. I supposed the plant threads only could become real with the appropriate mental energy from humans.

I was building an obsession upon the sources of the threads, the material of the threads, and the process by which the threads united and were wrapped to become a skein that transported human consciousness. But I did not know where or how to move forward.

I needed to take a break. Blackwood's short stories book was on my desk. I opened it. His arcane interpretations of the landscape always forced me to think differently.

In the table of contents a particular short story caught my attention, *Descent into Egypt*. For the last six years Egypt had just been on the other side of the Red Sea from my home. And

Yenbo port was the connection—to Africa, to Egypt.

So, I started reading—and couldn't put it down.

It was almost 8PM when I finished it. I was dizzy. Books always have taken me to gardens of the imagination.

Unfortunately, neither in Blackwood nor my own thinking had I found a technique to enable the weaving of the threads of spirituality, design and landscape, not to speak of wrapping skeins. But hunger shook common sense back to the foreground. I headed over to the stubbe.

***

Kurt Says

In that last section where CJ talks about his explorations into the hoped-for intersection of spirituality, design, music and landscape, I must admit, he created in me a positive hope for his success. He made it seem logical. That's what I've been looking for! Landscape architecture design should have the potential to convey "effulgences" to users.

There is no doubt that CJ was moving landscape architecture design beyond the classic design elements and principles taught at every university. While the practical side of me says "no way", I still hold onto my selfish design-breakthrough hope.

Let me look again at CJ's mysterious disappearance and death in Cairo. I have two points to make. First, from his above writing, he was on fire in his design search. Suicide has to be ruled out. Second, CJ's reference to the Algernon Blackwood story, *Descent into Egypt*, in my opinion, was a clue. I read the Blackwood story. It was all about music, the landscape and high culture. That observation was the clue. It showed me that CJ had a deep landscape/music/design reason for going to Egypt.

He already had that design interest before he was offered a job in Cairo. Could he have intentionally disappeared? I wish I had his writings, if he made any, from his time in Cairo.

I am actually surprised he left the Swiss Alps for Cairo. He was all in on that Jungfrau Region landscape. And the more I think about it, the more I am thinking that CJ must be on some kind of walkabout. But I have no evidence, no proof, just a strong hunch.

5-The Tals

Tourism

...in CJ's own words...

The tals? I visited them both. Lauterbrunnental, Grindelwaldtal. Tal means valley. The Lauterbrunnen Valley was different from the Grindelwald Valley. After a long and turning run through steep, nearly V-shaped topography, covered by thick forests lightly sprinkled at the bottom with open meadows, Grindelwaldtal had finally at its head a large, broad, open bowl with plenty of pasture land. Lauterbrunnental was short and narrow. It was U-shaped with pasture lands only on the very bottom and both sides dominated by tall, steep, vertical cliffs.

But these geophysical details did not consume me. Rather it was the special energy of this region.

These were the two valleys that Ed had first described to me. Valleys that inspired Tolkien! How special. How unique. From what powerful source?! Musicians, authors, poets, all have had each their own interpretations of the unique inspirational qualities of this Jungfrau Region.

As I walked to the stubbe, the mountains drove my imagination—super scale—super energy—I lived the inspiration like it was a powerful melody and I was riding it.

I didn't even know I was walking. I was being.

But it was my appetite that had driven me back to the stubbe. When I arrived, the Blumisalp stubbe was buzzing. The terrace was full. The long tables were noisy. And Suzie was busy behind the bar.

I said hello to her, asked if her friend from Lauterbrunnen was in.

She said, "No, not yet. Later, I'm sure. You say you were hungry? That's good. There's a group of people sharing a fondue at one of the long tables. You should join them. Have you had fondue?"

"What?"

"Fondue. It's a Swiss tradition—melted cheese and wine in a communal pot heated from beneath by a candle. The table is supplied with baskets of bite size pieces of bread that each person dips into the melted cheese pot with individual long-stemmed forks. Heard of it before?"

I said, "No, but I could eat a horse, point me in the right direction."

Suzie handed me a long-stemmed fork and pointed out the long table with three fondue pots. Then she walked me over to one of the long tables, and said, "Let me introduce you to them. They are professionals, the regional tourism staff. They all speak English and they all are into the landscape."

"CJ, this is Thomas, he is the Director of Tourism here in Grindelwald. Thomas, CJ is a landscape architect from Saudi Arabia. He's been mesmerized by the Grindelwald landscape. Maybe you two have some things in common?"

Suzie went back to the bar. I sat down next to Thomas and asked, "What's going on today?"

Thomas said, "We have a new employee, so we welcome him to the team."

After Thomas introduced me to the team, I asked Thomas what the goal of his office was. Thomas said, "Our goal is to keep the magnet on all traditional and emerging tourist groups. We want to assure that all have their expectations satisfied. And we must increase return guests."

I had questions. "I just can't see how you can begin to satisfy the diversity of your international crowd of tourists... unless they are all like me... mesmerized by the landscape... then they just need a clean bed and good food..." I finished by sharing a warm, personable smile with all at the table. I thought of myself as open minded but in the face of these number crunchers,

144

marketing smooth talkers and regulatory desk jockeys, I felt, dare I say, bored with the content. I took my fork, stabbed a piece of bread dug into the fondue—washed it down with zwickel. And again!

One of Thomas' staff members said, "With this Jungfrau landscape, we have what Antoine Watteau called *une fête galante*. We have an extraordinary scene of idyllic and bucolic charm."

I was respectful to the people but all-American as I kept digging into the fondue.

Thomas continued, "He is right." But, before he could say anything further, up came a lady Thomas obviously knew well. He immediately stopped talking, stood up... they greeted each other with kisses on the cheeks, three times. She sat down next to Thomas and he introduced her to me as Christina. She was Director of Mountain Research in the Institute of Geography at the University of Bern. Since the early 1990s, she had helped build the natural and cultural geographic databases to support the bid for the Aletsch Glacier to gain UNESCO World Cultural Heritage status.

With her *stang*, she came over next to me and sat down asking, "What brought you here?"

I paused from mining the fondue pot and answered, "Pleased to meet you. I'm a landscape person... landscapes, from the extensive geologic scale of geography and planning, to the intensive backyard vegetable garden scale of design and daily interaction. I'm an American landscape architect. That's what I do... and that's why I came to the Jungfrau Region... to experience the special nature, the special energy of this landscape. What I find is that the closer I get to it, the more diverse it is, the more windows and doors reveal themselves for exploration and the more questions I have."

I noted her interest and continued, "You, Christina, you have been assembling data from this region for what, ten years? And oh, by the way, I met an American guy on my way in, the other day, named Ed, on the train out of Bern. He told me he was doing landscape research with UNESCO and the University of Bern, maybe you know him?"

"Yes, yes, yes, we work with a consultant researcher. Ed, Ed Scheider; but to get to your research question, we have been on this project... to be exact, fourteen years. We began in 1992. There were lots of bits everywhere, digital and analogue. Written records, recordings, oral histories, photos, artwork, a broad spectrum of archives. Individually well kept, but not at all cross referenced, or accessible to the public at large. We have historical aerial photos beginning from over a hundred years ago. We are putting all into one easily accessible database."

"That's amazing!" I said.

I took another couple stabs of bread, dipped into the fondue as she continued, "Regarding the management of the landscape, this might surprise you. There are written records in this Grindelwald Valley region, *taleinungsbrief und friedhags*, going back nearly seven hundred years. Essentially they are the record of human management of this landscape so that they did not abuse its ability to support their families and communities."

I was still digging into the fondue as she paused. I politely asked, "I imagine it has always been a substantial challenge, to not wear the landscape out over these years... steep slopes, forests, cliffs, pastures, population growth... is it not?"

My stomach said enough fondue. I washed down with Zwickel and listened to Christina.

"It is a testimony to human civilization, CJ, that under the burden of survival, the people, on their own, have gotten together and established a legacy of sustainability over seven centuries."

"Now, that is sustainability that I can get behind," I said. "That works for me. But this whole tourist invasion, what, going back two hundred years and now causing a much greater density of human habitation... has the balance been upset and how did it get started in the first place?"

Thomas said, "We work closely with the UniBern studies and the UNESCO management programs. We align our tourism targets so as to not erode, to not injure or damage the regional 'life giving' cultural and landscape roots."

Christina continued, "He is right. This area, the gross

number of square kilometres gets no larger, so the coordination is essential, evolution of uses is essential. For example, during the Little Ice Age, the glaciers pushed into the valley, severely reducing directly adjacent arable land. The locals adjusted to maintain income by cutting and transporting large blocks of ice to larger cities in need, some as far as Paris."

"But what about tourism?" I reminded. The conversation, though interesting, was not as filling as the fondue and beer. The last 36 hours had been a super re-charge on so many levels in this landscape that this table conversation just did not have any juice in it. Too academic—too many numbers and dates—I had gathered a visceral taste from these mountains and the people living in them that made this discussion... just dry.

Christina said, "It is important to remember, to imagine the communications domain two hundred years ago, handwritten and carried at horse speed, on poor roads, through dangerous countryside. Multiple impressions and opinions did not get analyzed together easily, except over much longer periods of time. The ice business got the word out about the region, its amazing glaciers and landscapes. Before long, on the words of Rousseau, Goethe, Wordsworth, and later Byron came their friends, musicians, composers and artists. Renaissance scientists like Albrecht von Haller, and later, Candole, and so many others. Over time word slowly filtered out via many different channels. In the nineteenth century the Jungfrau became 'the' place to visit for the 'who's who' in Europe. Interlaken became the focus... then the climbers. That is how it all started."

She had more to add, "In the twelfth century, at Interlaken there was established an Augustinian Order of the Canons Regular. Its purpose was to take care of travellers on their way to and from Rome and the Holy Land. One could argue that as the beginning of regional tourism, don't you agree, Thomas?"

He said, "Definitely, in an academic sense. The buildings are still there in Interlaken. But for us here in Grindelwald, we seek something more immediate with future perspective. But we all agree that landscape roots, physical and especially cultural, run deep."

147

Christina said, "The morals and ethics of the Order of the Canons Regular presaged the Reformation. They established a long tradition in this region of austerity, renunciation, chastity, energy devoted to God, concern and care of the soul... rather than private property acquisition. There has always been a unique balance between church domination and individual freedom here. In this region, over the centuries, there is a kind of ebb and flow. People are religious but they know only their own hard work can assure their family security and survival."

Then she said, "As far as balance, we as planners and archivists, the farmers, everyone works hard to keep, to maintain the excellent visual, cultural, ecological and agricultural health of the landscape. Those are the roots that feed the future."

On and on the explanation went. Some of it was interesting; but gradually, the din in the Stubbe overwhelmed our tourism conversation. Fogged by tedium, both verbal and mental, I excused myself to stretch and stepped out onto the terrace.

***

Night with the Kings

...in CJ's own words...

Free from the stubbe din, the outside was good... it was large and full. The night air carried a refreshing visceral energy that was totally missing from that long table tourism conversation.

On the outer edge of the stubbe terrace, I stood looking across at the massive dark mountains directly in front of me. The moon had not yet risen in this bowl of a valley. I wondered. It felt like a mystery... the mountain presence... my closeness... I could almost grasp it; but every time it seemed just about accessible, it became unreachable. It was more than I wanted to try to unbundle. It was too large.

Too powerful. It gave out its breadcrumbs at its own pleasure. And I was happy to take each breadcrumb and resolve it into my design quest. That was my simple human endeavour. And something I felt in the mountains was... God-like. Beyond description. But I tried. I let my imagination run free.

The mountains had a look. Impenetrable, impenetrable to humans, that was the look... the feel. Superscaled to humans, a presence that warped my perceptions of both time and space... a presence that warped my thoughts... warped my mind... warped my senses. I continued stirring my thoughts... in a strange sort of nighttime wondering... might this have been the realm... I had a funny thought... of giants? A strange thought it was, but certainly appropriate for the scale of this landscape. These mountains had some kind of huge spirit about them, in them, through them.

Suzie taught me, in conversation and through the people she had introduced to me, the incredibly diverse realities of these mountains. Thanks to her, I had learned about the mountains, deeply. I felt them. I shared with them. How could these mountains and the humans share? It was all too strange, all beyond any of my standard measurement tools and conventions. Feelings beyond emotions, beyond intellect. But somehow that all resulted in a growing inward strength. Strength I felt for my design quest.

My thoughts were interrupted by the words of Christina, who had just walked up next to me. She said, "Nice to have met you, CJ, I will be leaving now."

"No, please don't leave yet... I wondered why you, a German, came here to Switzerland to work?"

She looked at me, and appeared to be considering her response. "There are two reasons. Centuries upon centuries ago, in Celtic times, the Alemanni tribes came from my part of Germany to settle these parts of this region... that is the deep link. But, closer to the surface, it is about the importance of information transference. This area contains a major node of documented information about human interaction with landscape over nearly a millennium. This information cannot be lost. This is my work. We are building a database we call Crystal Vision, everything clearly visible from and for past, present and future."

She continued, "Here the people have developed a set of landscape values that assures the health of themselves and the landscape despite changing climate, despite changing technologies, despite changing social contexts. They have a landscape culture that is both practical and, in a sense metaphysical, larger than any short-term objectives, larger than generations."

This was not the entire story from Christina. She spoke to me with a frankness that surprised me. I thought maybe the beer had freed her circumspect professional observations. I can only summarize this perspective she shared by interpreting between the lines of our snippets of conversation through the

150

entire evening. The Germanic people had always looked at the mountain people in Switzerland as simple country folk. In pejorative American slang, "Rednecks". As such, Christina carried an almost innate supremacy in her university and regional database work in the Berner Oberland Jungfrau Region.

I asked, "Why is your job not being done by a Swiss?"

She answered, "My job was not one for country folk. In the beginning I maintained a collegial demeanour while working here. In time, especially after carefully reading the Grindelwalders' seven-century records of landscape management, I grew to have a grudging respect for these mountain people."

I was thinking about how hard agricultural work had not reduced the magnetism of this Jungfrau Region landscape when Christina said, "I have to go to catch the train."

"Sorry for all the questions, but just one more, please. What is it, this spirit of the landscape here... what is it, that still has an enthralling attraction to outsiders, as well as locals... do you have any metric for that, yet?"

"I am not sure it is measurable with any tools, yet. We look at all economic, environmental and cultural groups and sub-groups. We cross reference surveys, responses, run them through different Geographic Information Systems models and multiple calibrations. Yet all we can conclude is that the landscape has both social and natural values. And we have to blend data in an ongoing effort of coordination. But how to design a blending system? And, what is being saved? What is being nurtured? There is still work to be done. Here is my card, CJ. Stop in to see me at UniBern if you are in town. I will show you the research; but tonight, I must go. Cheers."

"Thanks, Christina, it's been my pleasure to speak with you, g'night."

Christina hurried away. It was about 10PM. I turned and started back in to the stubbe. I paused at the door. The crowd had begun to thin.

***

Entheogenic

I walked across the stubbe. The players had changed. There were fewer people. The din had evaporated. The stubbe was restrained now.

I saw someone new at the bar talking with Suzie... a girl, a young lady, black toreadors, and a black short sleeve t-shirt, with the following printed on her back...unmistakably Helvetica font... "all your BASE are belong to us"... it was all lower case in white except BASE was upper case and in an energetically attractive, spring green colour.

When Suzie saw me, she smiled and motioned me over. She introduced, "CJ, this is Lumen Naturae. Everyone calls her Ellen, or LN, for short. She's my friend, a BASE jumper from Lauterbrunnen. You know about BASE jumpers, don't you, the people who jump from fixed objects like building, bridges or cliffs using a parachute?"

I nodded and she continued, "I tell you, if all the BASE crowd was like her, I'd still be in Lauterbrunnen."

Suzie continued, "LN, CJ is a landscape specialist who has spent his last six years, right?... in the arid Arabian Peninsula on the Red Sea coast."

During the introduction, I looked at LN. She was shortish, five foot four or five, in her mid-twenties. She had dark brunette hair, pixie cut... an athlete all the way. She was toned and taut of body everywhere, with longer legs gracefully carrying well proportioned, curvaceous hips, waist, breasts and shoulders... definitely on the pumped, muscular side; but with a soft delicateness... she could be a model... she wore no makeup... her eyes were hazel... clear, certain. On the front of her black t-shirt was another interesting bit of graphic text design. The words "Deep Green" were spelled out in OldSkool ascii art, spring green colour, and it was followed by some kind of smaller point, Helvetica font, white colour... looked like binary code.

I asked, "What does your t-shirt say?"

LN answered in a voice that was direct, yet soft, perfectly balancing the tautness of her physical presence, "Those are my initials in binary. BASE jumping—digital—electronics—I'm into them. Suzie told me that the landscape here has captured you, is that so?"

My smile was all affirmative.

"So, we definitely have landscape in common," she said.

I was not really up on the BASE scene. I looked at Suzie, and asked, "What did you mean when you said you left Lauterbrunnen because of the BASE jumpers?"

Suzie answered, "Look, a lot of them are cool, generally quiet, well focussed people... like LN; but the whole scene has attracted the groupies who are just like bad tourists... noisy, pretend adrenaline freaks, most of whom do not have the nature to jump themselves. They drink, they smoke, they make messes, they make noise, all to excess... bad tempered, fake pride, hubris all over. *C'est comme ça, n'est-ce pas*, LN?"

"Kind of, Suzie, especially about the hangers-on, the groupies; but the real BASE people are team people who, by their own choice, confront death by a hair and that is a seriously strange thing to share."

LN continued, "And, you know, they just need some good influence around them—to set a standard, by example—to teach them respect and how important respect is... which of course is, in the first place, what the whole BASE mentoring system is all about."

I asked, "Tell me, LN, how'd you get into BASE? Is it naturally part of what young folks from Lauterbrunnen do, or what?"

"Maybe Suzie has already told you that my family, Burgener,

153

has always been in these valleys. Our family name can be found in the Walliser, or Valais side of the Aletsch Gletscher, so we have long traditions with the mountains.

"In my family there are five kids. I was born third, the only daughter. My mother taught me the kitchen, the gardens, and how to nurture the young ones. My father taught me the mountains as if I was a son... hiking, climbing, skiing, skating. He took me paragliding on his lap when I was young. It all seemed natural.

"I loved the climbing, the cliffs, the Big Nose in the Lauterbrunnental. My father showed me how. My brothers pushed me. They teased me, calling me '*kleine lutine*', little elf. I pushed myself to excel, to exceed. So sky diving came after paragliding; and BASE jumping was just the natural way down after climbing up.

"As BASE became more popular in Lauterbrunnen, it became important for Lauterbrunnen jumpers to mentor, to show respect by example—otherwise there is great danger because every exit and every drop zone is part of the landscape, and every part of the landscape is managed, has been managed for centuries. These places cannot be abused by disrespectful behavior. So I am a proctor or, a guardian of sorts, by my presence in the BASE scene."

"But," I wanted to know, "why do you do it? Why do you jump? What is it, just an adrenaline high?"

LN answered, "That's a deep subject, CJ. But it is a question we all ask. Let me try to answer your question this way." She chose her words slowly, carefully. "It's a face-to-face challenge with death, right here, right now. It's an 'all-in' thing. It's one person, one on one, against death, and that's an adrenaline rush in those certain seconds. But it's also team preparation, team learning, all around. In the end though, it's standing on my own two feet and preparing to meet all challenges in the face of... mistake equals death."

I felt a tad uncomfortable as I asked, "But death can come at any time to anyone, right?" I preferred the landscape of the external to the landscape of the internal. Before letting her answer, I rephrased the question, "I am interested to hear more

154

about this adrenaline high and if it has any relationship to the landscape energy in these mountains, what do you think?"

LN, clearly sensing my discomfort, said, "I'm a landscape person—climbing, paragliding, skydiving, all beautiful interactions with the landscape. BASE, well that's an exploration of the traditional landscape and the internal landscape—what is that window of adrenaline—what can I see... what can I find... it's a landscape exploration... in a strangely numinous, or spiritual beyond spiritual sense... what is it that makes us want more... makes us say, please don't let it end? What is it?"

"Amazing, window of adrenaline, I follow, absolutely amazing," I said, "... tell me more."

LN delved into the internal landscape, "That adrenaline experience has an academic side for me because my education has included plant science and pharmacology. At the university in Gottingen, I studied both Albrecht von Haller and Paracelsus to understand how the medicines have evolved... have evolved from the special magic of plants, plants that give comfort, that add comfort, soothing, beauty... and how students and researchers of medicine have addressed the early alchemy and contemporary chemistry that comes from plants in the landscape... and how people use them. What are people looking for in churches, in alchemy, in life, and what is that adrenaline experience that makes it so attractive, so challenging?"

She paused, then continued, "I look at those kinds of experiences as real life entheogenic experiences—things that bring me closer to God—positive things—almost medicinal— hopeful—and if managed carefully, they can be healing to the dire condition of human life."

LN sounded like she had been to a similar door that I had visited long ago; but she was upbeat. I asked, "Answers—LN, any answers?"

She said, "Maybe we all choose to explore till that final door of death which, in and of itself, is also an exploration... maybe we find something along the way... but we all explore only according to our own capabilities."

***

Deep Green

...in CJ's own words...

I changed the subject. "Can I ask you about something lighter, something that Suzie and I talked about earlier..."

"Sure, what is it?"

"LN, you are modern; but your family has generations after generations the experience of these mountains. Hermann Hesse, in *Peter Camenzind*, seemed to be writing about families like yours... and he never said anything about... gnomes—Suzie told me that around here people call them *zwergs*. Tell me about gnomes, please. Are they inner? Outer? Real? Tourist business?"

"Mountain people like my family are blessed to be born and live in such a beautiful place, rich in plants, soil and water. There is a harmony of motifs, woven through all activities. In the days of my great-grandparents, life was all about agriculture, animals and weather. One of the few Swiss French writers translated into English, Ramuz, Charles Ferdinand Ramuz, wrote about the same time as Hesse; but Ramuz described in country folk words, just what farm life was—it was the same for us.

"As beautiful as the landscape is, we can hate it. As jolly as we can sing, we can suffer flagrant malaise. The full range of human emotions are in play. And maybe that's why the overall humanity level is quite healthy here in this region. Anyhow, about gnomes... gnomes are guardians of the balance, both moral and environmental. Not really different than parents

156

who, if their children behave badly, threaten them with bogeymen. There is no mystery; but..." Her voice trailed off.

"But what?" I asked.

"Really, the sagas are the sagas and they go back before written history... and who is your authority... even in the early 1800s there were stories of the Beatus Caves on the Thunersee having been the home of a dragon which Saint Beatus chased out before he made those caves his sanctuary. Others have said that those caves, and some outside Interlaken, deep down, lead as far as the Black Forest, as far as Franz Hartmann's Unterberg."

LN continued, "You know, if you go back three generations, word of mouth, the sagas start to morph and start to disintegrate; but it still is said that *zwerg*, gnome entries into the mountain caves, are invisible to all except the *zwerg*."

"So... LN, I'm confused... what do you think... they exist... they used to exist... they're just a TV show idea? Tell me."

"Okay, look. My botanical studies at Gottingen led me into many different cultures--including those from India. So, if you factor in such things as, according to ancient Indian, or Vedic history, the change in human perception in the Kali Yuga... if you factor in how little our current scientific understanding is of the underground and undersea of this earth... if you then ask yourself the question of gnomes as perhaps some life form that moved through solids in another yuga... a yuga where human capacity was so highly developed that even writing was not required... memory was strong... not disturbed as we are today... CJ, in my opinion, the jury is still out on gnomes."

I laughed... but inside I felt it was a hollow laugh. I was on some kind of uncomfortable edge between internal and external. LN looked at me, quizzically, and said, "You don't have to believe me; but let me remind you that for hundreds of years everybody lived comfortably thinking that this world was flat and the sun revolved around it... similarly the work of Paracelsus, of Boehme's *'Signatura rerum'*, of von Haller, of Hartmann... their science holds, at its roots, observations from the past that do not fully coincide with popular science these days... and, who knows what discovery may cause a rethink, a recovery of past knowledge, a reordering of past knowledge to give us a softer 'hard science', a softer 'technology' around which to organize our daily lives, without giving up the advances that have reduced our day-to-day, season-to-season dependence on weather and other natural events?"

I said, "Those are really some macro landscape issues."

We all went quiet. LN excused herself and left the bar. I appreciated the pause, drained my *stang*. Suzie and her helper were busy cleaning up.

I thought, Suzie and LN were a couple of beautiful and special women. Suzie had a power, a way of using her innate attractiveness to influence other people in discussion, she had a softness in her aura. LN also had beauty; but she had a strength—a powerful aura, a natural born leader.

As I was thinking, I watched LN walk to the rest rooms. I noted that the heels of her low-cut shoes had reflective logos on them. I asked Suzie.

She answered, "That reflective logo is the shield, the Lauterbrunnen coat of arms. It says, 'Lauterbrunnen'."

I asked, "...and what's with that on the back of her neck... was that a tattoo? Did I see a bright green skull and crossbones there?"

"You'd better ask LN about that when she gets back. She runs with a bunch of international groups, John Zerzan groups, the whole green anarcho-primitivism thing... she works with them the same way as with BASE jumpers..."

I interrupted, "Zerzan, anarcho-primitivism... what?"

"CJ, this region is very much into small scale local production. Maybe it is a combination of a long history of self-survival and extreme topography. That's what you and I talked about the night of the yodellers—people here take care of themselves and the landscape—it is the tradition. And the youth are into it."

These were threads in many conversations that hinted at landscape connections of which I had no experience. I thought the same back in Ban Muang when Vrndadevi delved into their deep approach to permaculture. She had summarized for me that it was all about individual liberty—the freedom to live and to locally earn their own living.

I was lost in those thoughts when Suzie said, "LN mentors... she's far from an anarchist, but has sympathies for some of their intentions. She tries to guide, to share her skills. You know, CJ, LN might be one of those people, called Indigo."

"Indigo, indigo what? That's a new one for me!"

"Indigo is a type of person with psychic strength, with powers that, how do they say, make them take strong positions and make strong statements against statism, against things like the so-called new world order; and yet, they are easily liked by the people they try to change. Maybe you could say she and some of her friends are the current version of freedom fighters, digital green freedom fighters."

My eyes showed Suzie my amazement hearing this about LN.

LN came back. When she came into my vision, I recalled, "...oh LN, is that a green tattoo on the back of your neck?"

"Interesting, no?" said LN. "I'm all about communicating, teamwork... there are so many things that get in the way of people successfully communicating... I use hints, little pieces of code that indicate things that are important to me... tags..."

She continued, "Yeah, that's a tattoo, a green tattoo, see the words beneath the skull and crossbones, take a look. DeepGreen. It's about Swiss independence, which is working toward a common goal but with the ultimate independence— no, it is not anarchy—but, to me, DeepGreen means no fear, it means do what you can to improve consciousness of the landscape, stewardship of the land—it follows from Earth First!—but it's not destructive—rather it's informative. Green skull and crossbones—people ask—I say green does not stop with death—it is the ultimate in recycling—about communication. Just like I use my climbing skills to mentor people who need to learn climbing skills. It's a follow on to the BASE mentoring tradition. The tattoo opens a discussion."

I added, "I can't help comparing your real-life landscape interactions with my own recent experiences of landscape. Here, if I understand correctly, it is all about a shared flow of life energies between humans and the landscape. But, everywhere and most everything I do and read about my profession, landscape architecture, the landscape is either a commodity, or someone's personal canvas... a fashion accessory... or a disposable asset... or worse, an ignored something out there somewhere... totally outside of consciousness... I guess I am looking for some middle ground but..." My voice tailed off.

It was late. Only the three of us were left in the stubbe.

I said, "Tonight has been great, in fact, the time here in the stubbe and in Grindelwald has been spectacular for me... a reawakening of what I first felt was important in the landscape and more. Wonderful! Look, it's after 11PM, and ladies, this has been real fun! But that is all tonight. I must do some writing."

I shook hands with LN, through her warm hand I felt a connection. I said, "It was a pleasure to meet and speak with you." Without a pause, I said to both, "I've got to call it a night. Thank you ever so much for your great landscape insights and conversation. Maybe we can get together another time. Good night." I left.

***

The Seeking

...in CJ's own words...

I t was dark, cool, crisp and quiet as I walked back to the hotel. And once again, the only sounds I could hear were my own footsteps on the pavement. No one else was out. I saw a gazillion stars in the sky. But I was tired... bushed from the early morning rise... bushed from the mountain walk. Tired though I was, I had to write notes from my walk, and from my conversations. Back in my hotel room, I sat down and began writing.

Suzie and LN were in my head. They were landscape people. They were mountain people. But LN... tagging... anarchist... couldn't be. I thought about my time in Switzerland—riding the trains Geneva to Bern to Zurich back to Bern then to Interlaken and finally to Grindelwald. I had a theory—a theory about graffiti and tagging and big cities and antifa anarchists. The graffiti and tagging was most intense in the big cities— London, Amsterdam, Brussels. Then as I travelled out to the countryside, the defacements decreased. I called it symptoms of cultural disease—a cultural disease with viral vectors. These viral vectors were primarily a young generation who had no idea of the hard work and dedication over decades, over centuries, required to achieve the material wealth they now took advantage of. Ruedi had said it was negative misdirected energy in the cities. Out here, it was pure, inspiring energy. My parents used to talk about silver spoon liberals. These taggers and graffiti "artists" were silver spoon anarchists.

In Switzerland I saw the same. Graffiti and tagging of the most intense along the railroad lines in Geneva, Bern and Zurich. In Geneva it even moved onto the public streets—not as bad as in Amsterdam and Brussels. And I did see tagging, ACAB and Antifa, ironically the most fascist, as I passed through Interlaken. I wondered, is the anarchy disease already taking root in Interlaken? I saw none in Grindelwald. But LN? Naw. Couldn't be. In love with a small-scale agricultural landscape and anarchy? They don't mix.

Anyhow I was tired. Decided to get into the design and landscape stuff in the morning. I showered and fell fast asleep. I dreamt all night. Design was unrequited drama in every dream.

I ordered orange juice, coffee and croissants for breakfast in my room. But my dreams hung on like a bad hangover. Cocoons? Real life? I woke up in a tizzy and could not get free. Took a long drink of coffee. Stepped out on my balcony, inhaled deeply and marvelled at the majestic mountains standing over me.

The tizzy? I needed to unravel it all. Starting at university, I had an obsession with design. How and why? Because it was treated as some kind of secular god. Nobody could define it, even though everyone was teaching it.

I concluded it was therefore like beauty... definition of design... in the eye of the beholder. Then I went on to find for myself what "my design" should be. Somehow, I intuitively knew that the plants had to be important. And I spent a lot of time in touch with classic fine arts and contemporary theory. I broadened myself.

My time in Tangier was instructive. I loved the hunt. The hunt, the quest, became a cocoon—a design cocoon wherein I could shelter from the threatening street culture and be constantly exploring. And in Tangier, I learned more about the importance of plants. On my way there, my visits to Brussels, Bilbao and Granada strengthened my appreciation of architecture, its decoration and the movement through it.

As I developed professionally, events in life required a cocoon. The design and project work cocoon protected me from the hurt of my loss. Then Vrndadevi told me what I was really searching for was knowledge of the absolute. But I continued on my design quest, even though the reality of real-life jobs had foiled my design aspirations.

But in Switzerland, I felt I was so close to a mature and replicable approach to design I had to dig deeply into it. As I was looking at all I had heard, all I had learned about the landscape of the Jungfrau Region in the Berner Oberland, I started wondering a couple things. What might I find? And if I find it, then what? I was stymied. Was I searching for the Holy Grail of design? Of landscape? Maybe Vrndadevi was right, I was searching for knowledge of the God, no matter what God's name.

I drank the rest of my coffee and went out on the terrace again. The power was there. I watched the sun's shadows move across the rock outcrops and forested gullies. Symphonic vision—watching gave me so much pleasure. It was a pleasure I could inhale. Rejuvenation. I went back inside and tried to put together this incredible jigsaw puzzle of ideas and realizations. I was sure that in that resolution I would find the missing key to my design quest—how to design so I could make sure that people could experience transcendent effulgences in my gardens and landscapes.

As I reviewed my design journal notes, I found that in addition to my own intimate Berner Oberland landscape experiences, I had the observation of seven other people in the past two weeks who felt the landscape power of these mountains. Surely the key must be in there somewhere. So I went through them, one by one.

It was funny. I had not even planned to be in Switzerland; but my hunt for Kaytee on behalf of Gordie changed everything. Then Vrndadevi, after telling me my design and project work cocoon was just a surrogate for my existential thirst for knowledge of God, knowledge of the absolute she called it, told me about the Swiss landscape.

She said, since I was going to Switzerland, I should be aware that the Swiss landscape has for many writers, musicians, men of letters been a source of inspiration. She lent me a couple

163

books, Mann's *Magic Mountain* and Hesse's *Peter Camenzind*. That got me started. The trip to Switzerland not simply a quest for Kaytee but as a design quest.

Magic Mountain's Hans Castorp felt the power in the mountain landscape; but he was confused about it—maybe that set me up for my own confusion that I struggled to resolve. And what about *Peter Camenzind?* The big modern urban world did him in and he took refuge in the small personal details of life in the mountains. Maybe I missed the clues there. Maybe I had been trying too hard to make the details applicable to all things?

Then when I finally got to Geneva, it was at the bookstore where I saw for the first time the images of the Jungfrau Region in the Berner Oberland. They absolutely enthralled me.

And then Ruedi. What about Ruedi? He was some kind of humorous, I might say, mystical character. He spoke non-stop about negative energy in the cities which according to him was the result of the people losing contact with the landscape. The power or the energy in the landscape, especially in certain regions of the Berner Oberland. He enthused me to go see and feel it for myself. And I did. And it happened.

But as enjoyable and powerful as my personal experiences of that energy in the landscape—I called my experience of transcendent effulgence—I could not put words or process to their understanding. So I vowed to seek deeper. I looked back on the days themselves. The day I journeyed for the first time to the Jungfrau Region in the Berner Oberland.

***

The Sought

...in CJ's own words...

There was Ed, the American on the train from Bern to Spiez. We spoke the same language—both from the USA. The same cultural language. He shared numerous details about the people and landscape of the Berner Oberland. Although listening to him was like reading a Wikipedia entry, he did leave a distinct impression. The Berner Oberland landscape was filled with strange powers and mysteries. After I'd been there a week, it was nothing I did not already experience myself. The power, the energy and the mysteries? I was trying to understand, to solve them.

In Grindelwald I had the good fortune to meet Suzie, a French expatriate from Corsica whose life had been built around mountains. The bottom line from her was that these mountains in our face in Grindelwald had an unusually pleasant vibe. Then she took me and my quest under her wing and introduced me to local people.

But none of them were quite like the Scot expatriate. Ian took me on a hike into the heart of mountain country—above the Gletscherschlucht in a scree left by a receding glacier between the mountain peaks of the Eiger, Monch and Schreckhorn. There I heard the mountains and the streams. Unimaginable resonance. No human civilization presence. In the silence, there was no silence. What was the point? Hearing. I had been that day in some arcane domain.

And hearing also was the point of the yodellers. People

whose lives had been part of these mountains—as had been their families—for generations. They sang of their love, their glorious attachment and the very nature of life in these mountains. I heard it though I did not understand their language. I felt the love in their a cappella singing. It must be something simultaneously coming from the each of the hearts of the singers—something like I felt on the Thunersee when I "saw" an unusual bidirectional energy exchange between the sky and earth via the rain.

Only with the yodellers it was between them and the landscape... some kind of exchange. Of what material is that energy exchange? Question. But what propelled me further into seeking? Mysteries without threat. I was seeking the answers to a mystery that was like a healing salve, whose very aroma started the healing. That was where I was with the landscape mystery in front of me in the Berner Oberland. The aroma propelled me. I needed the answer. I needed the real thing.

I had a myriad of large landscape experiences in the Berner Oberland. They all related to the three most important:

1. The sequence of spaces, landscape rooms through which I moved from Bern to Grindelwald;
2. The ecstatic transcendent effulgence I experienced in the Grindelwald cemetery; and,
3. The similar transcendent experience I felt when I heard the yodellers.

Those three were the most intense and most "eye" opening. I felt things from each of those three experiences that were mysterious, beyond words. But these experiences were similar to what I had felt in the Obelisk Garden in Ban Muang and in my Tangier gardens. Those were my starting points.

In Switzerland, those were the three paths I needed to follow. Those were the clues that I hoped would bring my design quest to fruition.

It was almost lunchtime. Time to refresh. I stepped out on the terrace. Did an IMAX review of the mountains—the equivalent of a deep breath with my eyes. Then I took a couple actual deep breaths. I was hoping the mountain magic would reappear. Didn't, so I went downstairs to the hotel stubbe and asked for a local cheese sandwich and Zwickel, unfiltered beer brewed locally.

I sat in the stubbe by myself and relished my lunch. After I finished I went up to the bar and asked if they had any regional specialty to finish off my lunch. They suggested a hay brandy. They opened the bottle and offered it to my nose. It was the fragrance of just cut pasture as I had smelled from the cemetery. They told me the history and said they sold small gift boxes with half litres and 1dl glasses. I bought the gift box and took it up to my room.

In my room, opened the bottle, poured a glass and went out on the balcony. Relished its softness. I asked myself, what was I seeking? Answer came in two parts. The first—what exactly was that feeling that I had experienced a couple times here. And second—how could I design to include it in my work.

As I thought about the first task, I remembered way back on the bike trip in Europe before Tangier. There was a guy named Bo. English guy studying architecture. He talked about that feeling when material transforms into spiritual as the goal of all great artists and architects. Funny, I thought, I had two decades of professional practice behind me including all the great professionals in LA and internationals from Yenbo; and I had never heard that kind of discussion. The real world versus the dream world? Yet here I was thinking I was on the verge of understanding it.

I thought about the professionals I had just met—Thomas and Christina, the tourism professionals. They lived and worked with the landscape. I thought about how their success was managed by numbers of tourists and frequency of returns. But then I thought... regulations—the bane of my design life in SoCal. I wondered if the reason why each little village had certain materials, certain coloured shutters and roofs, was they were obligated by regulatory requirements. Hmmm— good thing or bad thing?

I remember the long talk I had with the database specialist,

Christina. How, at the end, she admitted they had no idea after analysis of centuries of historical data using all the most modern modelling software... no idea how to measure the special attractiveness, the special power of this region. What was I hoping for? Was this the needle in the haystack? Was I really searching for the holy grail of landscape design? Fool's errand?

I sipped on the hay brandy and thought. Then I remembered Rory. There was something I liked about his simple, straightforward enjoyment of the Berner Oberland landscape. It satisfied his senses. Finished. Didn't have anything to do with transcendent anything. Again, I wondered if I was looking too hard.

Then there was Peter, Uncle Alp. What was it he said? Cherish the *alp*. Fear the *berg*. It summed up his life, no? In six words? Should I try to extract a secret from those six words? I poured myself a second glass of hay brandy.

I was trying to learn how people were living with this land for in that must lie some clues. LN said some interesting things about famous Swiss alchemists and what they were searching for a couple centuries ago, before the "enlightenment". They didn't find the magic but they were all over the plants. They thought the keys were in the plants. Maybe it is the same for my search. Thinking about it, I remembered that is exactly what Fyodor and Tolly were telling me in Tangier at the Hibiscus House.

As I took another sip of hay brandy, Tolly's explanation of strange plant mirrors came back to me. He said something like, "Plants in the garden or in the landscape can become some kind of magical four-dimensional mirror, unique to each human looking at them." And I thought that was exactly what I learned from this Jungfrau Region Berner Oberland landscape.

I poured one more glass of hay brandy and went out on the balcony. I sat down and rested my thoughts.

I wasn't there yet. But I stopped worrying. I went back inside and saw Algernon Blackwood's short stories. I had left a bookmark on his story *Descent into Egypt*. It was a story about a man who was searching for the attractive, for the hidden. Answers for things larger than time. I decided to read it again as the sun was setting on the day, reflecting off the faces of these great mountains.

It was pitch black by the time I finished. The book came from Suzie and this story gave me a strange yearning, a strange excitement that maybe what I was seeking was buried in the past but that I would have to give up something of great value in the present if I wanted that knowledge. I washed my face with cold water and headed over to the Stubbe, looking for Suzie.

***

Rasta?

...in CJ's own words...

I took a quote from Blackwood's story—something to share with Suzie. I wanted to hear her opinion. The quote? "The desert slipped in through walls and ceiling, rising from beneath our feet, settling about us, listening, peering, waiting." I wondered if that could be how the Jungfrau Region Berner Oberland landscape creates its aura around people. And what exactly could be that aura—physical, emotional, spiritual?

She was busy when I came into the stubbe. So, I took a seat at the end of the bar where I could watch all the tables and all those entering and leaving. She waved to me and indicated she would be free shortly. I crowd-watched.

It was then that I had the strangest feeling, when my eyes fell on a woman sitting by herself at the far end of one of the long tables. The stubbe was busy and most all the seats were taken. The crowd was mixed—some jovial, some discreet, but all relaxed and having enjoyable civilized times.

But the woman sitting by herself... a magnet for my eyes... and more. But more? What? I did not know. She had a Rastafarian cap bulging with hair and a tie-dyed yellow, green and white T-shirt over a pair of blue jeans. She was looking out toward the mountains so I could not see her face. How did I know it was a she? Her side profile revealed a chest that could only be that of a well-endowed woman.

And then Suzie was next to me.

She asked, "What can I get you?"

"Huh, what?"

"Do you want a Zwickel?"

"Yeah, *stang*, please."

She brought my beer and asked, "You in a daze?"

I said, "Who's that Rasta lady by herself at the end of the middle long table?"

Suzie said, "Oh, her? She's been a regular here for a couple years—why do you ask?"

"Something familiar about her..."

"Listen, CJ, you don't want to get into that."

"Why?"

"We all call her Mahboula, a name given to her a few years ago by a Kuwaiti guy who stayed with her for a month or two."

"Okay, now I am interested... tell me more."

"Mahboula means crazy woman. She's a wilding."

"Wilding?" I asked.

"Wilding is 'off-the-edge' socially. She lets any stranger into her house—need I say more?"

"She lives way out on the edge of town. She comes into town once in a lunar month—on the hunt for a male, any male. I hear it is usually one-night stuff. She comes in with her Rasta cap—sits for a while looking over the crowd. Then she takes off her cap. Look, she's doing that now."

I saw the lady's long red Rasta locks come tumbling out as she stood up and shook them. I watched electricity ring like a bell from her flowing hair—stunning. She did look familiar. I thought, wilding? Maybe I could learn something... maybe about how she sees the landscape. She had energy. Wilding? There has to be more to a "wilding" than a romp between the sheets.

I asked Suzie, "What does she drink?"

Suzie said, "She brings her own stuff. I heard she brews stuff at her place. She's weird, CJ."

I didn't hear Suzie. That Rasta lady had captivated me. She was still sitting by herself. I walked over and stood next her asking, "Mind if I sit?"

She turned to face me and in clear sight of her face, I saw everything. I remembered fully our night in Casablanca and our week studying Arabic. She had those strange stories about the Mediterranean and the Sahara.

I said, "Bree? Is that you?"

"CJ? How many years?"

"Maybe twenty since Morocco. The barkeep told me you have been here for a few years."

"Sit down and don't pay attention to that barkeep. She and her girlfriend have it in for me. They're afraid of me. It is a surprise to see you. We go back a long way. Do you have time to talk?"

"I've got all the time in the world."

"I remember it like yesterday. You listened to me before when I was in trouble in Morocco—not once but twice. Now, it's my turn. I owe you. I will listen to you. C'mon, let's walk to my place. Forty-five minutes at a good pace uphill."

"Yeah? Okay, let's do it."

The moon was near full. The sky cloudless. She led me past my hotel, past the cemetery, then on and on. She kept a good uphill pace—faster than Ian's the other day. She walked quietly and rarely spoke.

But she did point out geographic reference points—the mountains, the Shreckhorn, the upper Grindelwald glacier, the Wetterhorn. We must have walked in the dark for more than a half hour when she stopped.

She spoke softly to me about the local cultural landscape we were marching through. She said that there were radii of uses in the landscape. The first was close to town where many people, families and older couples walked. Then the next was where people walked their dogs, far enough from people that dog owners felt they could safely let their dogs off the leash. Walking to her place was beyond that dog walkers' zone—on a rarely used path.

We walked uphill quite a bit; but we never left the court of the kings. She said we were closer to Grosse Scheidegg than Grindelwald when we arrived at her place. We must have walked uphill 45 minutes. Her place sat on a small flat just away from a slope down to a rivulet feeding the Lutschine river. The rivulet burbled softly, sweetly.

On the outside, her place was unassuming. It looked like any other haybarn I'd seen dotting the entire valley. But they were usually surrounded by pasture. Hers was cosseted by shrubs and trees.

As I got closer, I could see some kind of garden with a lot of flowers glowing in the moonlight. I asked her about them as we walked under an arbour, overflowing with climbing white roses in full bloom. We paused under the roses. I could also smell the unmistakable scent of pinks, carnations, they were between the arbour and the door to her place.

She stood close to me. Her body was sweating, as was mine. She said, "Never mind the outside garden plants tonight. We'll look at them tomorrow. Let's go inside, I think we've earned a drink, some refreshment. The night is still young. We need to make up for a whole lot of lost time, don't we?" Then she unlocked and opened the door to her... haybarn?

***

Lost Time

...in CJ's own words...

She entered first and switched on a low wattage light that softly illuminated... I couldn't believe my eyes as I entered. It was no haybarn. Aromatic apothecary bunches of herbs hung in festoons.

"Haybarn?" I asked.

She said, "Used to be a haybarn; but I refurbished the inside while preserving the outside."

She offered me a simple wood straight-back chair near the centre of the room. There were only two chairs and a good-sized wooden table. As I sat down, Bree busied herself in the corner preparing what she called mead. She said, "Around back I keep bees and make local brew. It is so nice speaking English with you."

"What?"

"You know... I learned the basics of German and the local dialect here; but I really only have superficial communication—cultural differences. When we talk, because we both have deep roots in the USA, the communication is deep—haven't felt that in years."

"I am not surprised you learned the local dialect; if I remember correctly, you excelled in our Casablanca Darija stage—not many did. I follow what you say about the presence and absence of cultural roots—it has been that way for me in Saudi Arabia—I just stopped trying because there was nobody on the other end—no connection. So tell me more about here."

I asked, "How did you find this place—how did you end up here? And your garden, tell me about your garden."

"I've been here almost 10 years now. Worked as seasonal help at a farm nearby, animals, agriculture... I liked the place and the people were friendly in their own way... lots of hard work..."

"This place, are you renting, what? Did you find this place like it is?"

"It was run down when I found it. I had a bequeath from my sympathetic grandmother, she was Swiss, from my mother's side. It was not much, enough to buy and fix up this place but not enough for me to leave a bequeath. Anyhow, so when I was convinced by the landscape vibe here, I bought it and worked through the *gemeinde*, village government, as long as I paid for everything, to get connected for water, sewage, electricity."

"I respect your determination with local regulators to make it happen; but the garden, it immediately had a vibe that captured my attention, tell me about it."

"The garden? The garden is me and I am the garden. Captured your attention? Enchanted, you were enchanted—that's how I feel it."

I interrupted, "Connectivity? Internet? Cable?"

"No way—that's all artificial intelligence. I take my input face to face from the landscape and people."

"Weren't there any government regs?"

"Lots—but I learned the language, got a visa and after that it was easy. For this place, their only condition was to keep the externals so that it would fit in the landscape as it always had... even though I have water supplied I have a trough for mountain water just outside..."

"Best of both worlds?!"

"Definitely."

"But Suzie said you were wilding?"

"She has her opinions. Wilding? You knew me before. I haven't changed. I connect with the landscape in my own ways. Wildings? Yeah, there are some around. They are like hobos, well, kind of, from way back in our own country. Roger Miller sang a song once, King of the Road, I think—had some lines about men of means without means..." As she served me a mug of her homemade mead, she sang some of the lyrics.

"Here wildings don't ride trains, they walk—some are young but most are old-timers—they all know the landscape well. And they know sympathetic farmers—like me—I keep a box outdoors with non-spoilable food stuffs—unlocked—seasonal stuff. Sometimes I talk with them. They have strange landscape stories."

"Suzie said you visit the stubbe once a month?"

"Suzie again? Yeah, once a lunar month—the old 28-day cycle stuff. It's a bodily function thing, just like going to the toilet. I need the release and I don't keep a man. And I noticed you don't have a wedding ring. Want more mead?"

I didn't want to talk about my past. I took another mug of mead, sweet, spicy. Never tasted anything like it.

I looked around her room. The room had a feel... a combination of modern stainless steel with medieval wood. There was an upright stainless-steel modern Liebherr freezer-fridge next to a medium size slate-coloured Aga with induction top. In the middle of all the kitchen workspace, she had a large stainless-steel worktable with large double stainless-steel sink. But the rest?

Everything in wood. Built in wood shelves on all the wood walls. All with books, knickknacks, arcane stuff if I was to guess. Above the work area, I saw an all-sizes, messy collection of mortars and pestles. Next to the work area were knives. And everywhere, hanging from the ceiling, were dried plants, flowers, leaves, stems, roots. Everything looked like it was in process... for what? I couldn't guess.

Not far from where we sat was a small, working brazier in the centre of the room. It was made of stone, had a heavy-duty steel hood resting on stone pillars and had a triangular support holding a huge pot over the fire which only had the glow of embers.

Between two rows of bookcase was a doorway-wide gap that was covered with full length hanging plastic strips... like those ones used on doors in Spain to keep flies out.

I asked and she answered, "The other side? That's where I

sleep. Got a toilet, shower and a hot tub back there. Are you good with the mead? Can I pour you another?"

I took another. Refreshed me and made me feel good all over.

I said, "I'm starting to get some memories back from Morocco... strange times we shared... Casablanca... Tangier..."

She said, "I'll be right back." She went to her bedroom and came back bare-breasted, asking, "Do you remember these?"

Well, that took my breath away. I certainly did remember that night in hot sweaty Casablanca where she showed me her undeniably awesome assets. Except for her breasts, she had slimmed down—I thought lost all the baby fat but none of the breast meat—farm work had made her lean. I said, "You must be living well. You look amazing."

She said, "Come here and take me."

I didn't need to be invited twice. She led me to her bed and I took her with a tiger's passion. It was the first time in 10 years that I didn't pay for sex. It was the real thing. I pounded it out.

Afterwards she said, "Now it's my turn."

She climbed on top of me, straddled and rode me like a bucking bronco. She worked me over and over. Then she finally got where she wanted. I saw her smiles... getting fuller, broader... she started beaming, her face was glowing... and then the room exploded with her banshee-like screams of pleasure. I was wrung out. She was wrung out.

***

Talking It Through

It was daylight before we both regained consciousness. She and I showered. Then we shared her hot tub. I hadn't been so relaxed... I couldn't remember ever.

She said, "I've never forgotten that night we stayed up late in Casa. You listened to me like nobody ever has." She reached for my hand and gently kissed my ringless ring finger with submission. I felt it through and through.

Then she offered, "Now, I must listen to you. Tell me your story. I need to hear how you have become so intensely wrapped up—internally tighter than a drum. Talk to me. I am yours. Let me hear."

I told her about my work in Saudi Arabia and the Kaytee quest that brought me to Switzerland. When it was time to get out of the hot tub, we got dressed and she told me to continue talking while she had kitchen work to do. In the meantime she put out some homemade bread and jam which we ate and washed down with a warm coffee-like drink. She took a quick drink and went back to work at her counter. "Making a batch of biscuits, time for baking," she said.

After the biscuits finished baking she took them out to cool then we went outside to the garden. The day had dawned clear and as the sun had begun warming the Grindelwald bowl, it became clearer. The mountains were sharp. The air? Cool and clean. I could see the evergreen forest and the treeline above us. Around the edge of her haybarn was mixed deciduous and evergreen forest. And her haybarn sat in a Swiss *alp*, as Uncle Alp would describe.

It was almost noon when she brought a basket to do some harvesting. The garden was larger than I remembered from last night. And it was jolly. So many plants cheek by jowl. Classic cottage garden plants. Herbs, flowers, soft fruits, salads and vegetables—a real companion plant masterpiece.

We walked together. She talked about the gifts from nature—borage, lavender, sage, rosemary, calendula, salvia, thyme, mugwort, cowslips and of course the roses.

"Cowslips?" I asked.

"Primroses—look around the stone paving under that rose arbour by my front door," she said.

I looked and saw myriads of primroses in clumps and clusters, wedged in between the large, rough stone pavers and thriving around the edges. "*Primula vera?*"

"They are mixed. The taller yellow are cowslips, *Primula vera*. The shorter mixed colours are common primroses, *Primula vulgaris*. Aren't they joyful?" she said.

She was at home in the garden, as she spoke. I thought, at home? No, it was more than that—she was in the zone. Her words made that clear.

She said, "I hear music from these plants. Each has its own tune. Amazed... I am always amazed as each plant offers to me its natural bounties... I spend all of my days among them. I can't call them pets, but I call them partners. Together we glow. Together we face difficulties. Together we survive."

I was turning over so many thoughts—Vrndadevi—permaculture—even my Tangier garden portals.

I said to Bree, "As I listen to you describe your garden, it takes me back to portals, where humans via plant portals have a transcendent experience—something I always wanted to achieve through my design..."

Before I could finish that thought, Bree said "Why? Why all that design stuff? Wasn't your portal experience in Tangier something very personal? Intimately personal? What makes you think you can make that happen to somebody else? You as guru? You as translator? That sounds like hubris,

179

megalomania..."

I listened. Somehow her personal attack did not feel like a personal attack. Why? Perhaps there was too much truth in her words. I asked, "Tell me more about the music you hear in the garden?"

"It is a feedback, like when giving rubs to the back of the neck to dogs... or cats when they purr... some people call it plant magic with a k... for me... the closer I get to each plant, the sweeter the music, the flow, the refreshment... it is not something I take willy-nilly. I am out here every day, morning and evening, rain and shine through all the seasons working with them. Gifts from nature—that's what they give me."

She had a practical way of describing what I tried to describe transcendentally. Bo's search for the stairway to heaven and Tolly's description of multidimensional plant mirrors book-ended what Bree described. I was fascinated.

She showed me her wood pile, the bees, the water trough, an espaliered apricot and then an apple tree under which she had two chairs and a small table. I sat and she said, "Going in to get the biscuits, would you like some more mead?" Couldn't say no—seemed like her all-purpose drink.

Her biscuits had a variety of currants in them. She served them with strawberries she had just gathered from the garden. The apple tree had its own fragrance and the gardens in the midday sun added theirs. I drank the mead deeply.

I wanted to talk more about music, plants and landscape. "Two special experiences have captivated me here in Grindelwald—the positive vibe that fully overcame my pineal gland and the yodelling outside the Blumisalp Stubbe. Maybe I am stuck on trying to put words to them, on trying to objectify them..."

"Exactly, they are what they are. You are blessed to receive those feelings. Come with me, I have some work to do and I would like your help."

We went inside where she gathered up some seeds, a trowel and a bucket. Then we went back outside to her compost pile where she asked me to fill the bucket from the bottom of the pile. The compost was dark, rich and well broken down.

As I handed her my bucket of compost, she grabbed an almost empty sprinkling can and handed it to me. She was into her work and said, "I have a couple patches asking for plants so I'm going to take some cuttings. Fill the sprinkling can from that brook over there and bring it to where I'll be working."

The brook was small but had a good flow. I brought her the full sprinkling can where she was gathering some cuttings. When she finished, she led me to a couple small bare patches where she planned to plant the cuttings.

"Will you trowel a trench 8 inches deep and 24 inches long? We'll start with these cuttings. Fill the trench halfway with compost and then mix half of the rest of the soil so the filled trench is an inch below the adjacent soil. Now fill that inch with water. After it all soaks in, mound the remaining soil. Then I will set the cutting six inches deep and I'll do the final watering."

She took me to another patch where I was to spread an inch of compost and then trowel it into the top two inches of garden soil. She told me to trowel it all so all the soil clumps were no larger than a centimetre. Then she spread seed directly over the top and lightly dampened it with water from the sprinkling can. She pulled out a tightly webbed mat of jute mesh that she pegged down along the edges.

She asked, "How are you feeling after the garden work?"

"Refreshed—I'm good."

"And your girlfriend, whatever happened?"

"My girlfriend? That's a story—a long, sad story." I hesitated for a moment. Then the words flowed, my worst memories flowed.

For the first time ever, I recounted the whole story. The deaths of my wife and three young children in a traffic accident... the story came out slowly and painfully. It was impossible to tell the story without tears running down my cheeks... and shortage of breath. A couple times when I was in deep emotional deficit, Bree took my hand in hers and when she squeezed I felt strength returning to my words and thoughts.

Bree had a presence... she absorbed my emotional pain. She

was rescuing me, emotionally rescuing me. She emanated a soothing, almost a healing aura that made me feel... clean. And sitting under the tree full of ripening apples, looking out at the mountains and the Grindelwald bowl—refreshed, satisfied and inspired. I had not known such relaxation in years.

***

Who's Who

We talked forever that afternoon. She was glad to be speaking American English to an American. I learned about her as she learned about me. Our hearts and bodies had already bonded. Our spirits were alive. We were destined.

We already had, back in Tangier gardens, horticulture and landscape in common; but that was long ago. As we chatted, Bree offered her perspective on plants as healing, protection from demons, providers of auras, auras of good health. We talked about art and the history of glacial movement. In front of us were the upper and lower Grindelwald glaciers, now out of sight as they had been before the little ice age in the 17th century. And how in the 19th century they had pushed into the Grindelwald valley upsetting the pastoral landscapes, turning them into ice fields. Had nothing to do with man—the changing of the climate was obviously something larger than earth itself—the sun and other planetary influences.

All that led to our discussion of science, culture, ethnobotany and once again the landscape. And it was the landscape all about us that dwarfed our social ideas—our speculation. I recalled and shared with Bree, "This place is made by God; it is a mystery beyond price, untainted by evil, with extraordinary sense of peace and security."

That is what we both felt. We paused, tired of thinking, tired of talking. Recharging.

Resting under the apple tree, I was enjoying looking at her garden when I saw for the first time in a farther corner, an unplanted area—a fire pit surrounded by 5 or 6 tree stumps sawn to be seats. I asked. She said, "Sometimes a couple wildings visit and we sit by the fire all night. That is when the strange stories about Swiss mountains, forests, caves and caverns emerge."

"Why do they share stories with you? I thought they kept away from normal civilization..."

"You think I'm normal civilization?"

"No, but I feel close to you... and... that closeness feels like... normal—comfortable. Maybe I used the wrong words."

"I hear music from plants and I talk about it. The wildings understand and they too feel relaxed enough to talk about... what nobody else does or knows about the landscape—stuff about the local landscape too. They told me there is a story about caves and caverns in the Jungfrau Region that hold treasures gathered from the era of the Crusades—gold that was taken as tax for passage. Swiss farmers showed crusaders returning from the Middle East how to find and safely get through the mountain passes."

"You're right, that's a strange story... but what you said earlier about hearing music from plants..."

"It's not exactly hearing but feeling—the closer I get to the plants... the sweeter the music... it flows and refreshes... maybe it's a pineal gland thing... a feeling that flows and refreshes— when I am working with the plants..."

"What you describe is so similar to what Tolly and Fyodor were exploring at the Hibiscus House gardens in Tangier 20 years ago—hard for me to believe that their gardeners were part of that human trafficking..."

"Enough of that—what you and I have here today is so much more important. There is evil out there but you and I together have found, right here, a source of good. I think of it as deep magic, ancient wisdom—something simple and deeply fulfilling."

We sat quietly for quite a few minutes. Internally I was trying to work through everything that Bree had brought to me. I had to ask, "Am I seeing, sitting next to me, a white witch?"

She took my words in like a cool breeze on a warm day, answering, "Witch, that is funny language that people who don't feel that deep grace and beauty of plants use as shorthand to describe people whom they fear."

She continued, "I don't want to force you away from your own path but they, the plants, have become my allies, my family. That connection is telepathic, it is spiritual, it is fairylike, it is a heart song, it is the language of plants, the language of the forest. Plants cast spells. How do you think those strange things that happened to you with plants and flowers in Tangier happened? Pineal? No, the plants communicate in ways modern science cannot measure. Live it. Believe it. We are having this conversation why?"

"Why?" I wondered out loud.

"Because we both have shared these plant communications. Your Tangier portals—your Tangier portals were your entry to the land of Faery. It is a place where breathing is no longer breathing. No words either."

She was right. Did that mean I too was a witch? Didn't dwell on that—made my original witch question feel foolish.

Bree had more to say, "I am collecting gifts from nature. In my heart I am a Christian, but rather than church dogma, I listen to a voice of inner knowing. Let me explain... I am not trying to be my own guru... but like Celts before times and now... we don't really know. No names—no titles—I am finding a path via my inner knowledge, my heart, my soul—from the heart with love."

She paused. I was hearing her heart speak—she was revealing her soul.

She said, "I am not a member of a witches' club or cult. I am Bree, your lover. And we are out in the garden just drinking herb tea... just sitting under the apple tree... just talking."

I smiled, said nothing.

Bree asked, "Hungry?"

***

Long Overdue

...in CJ's own words...

To close off the workday, a late afternoon snack was on the cards. Bree sliced some *muetschli* (this year's mountain cheese) and bread which she served to me along with more mead and a tangy herb spread for the cheese sandwich. She said, "I have poured two small glasses of *johannesbeeren* wine. The people I worked for make it every year and give me a couple bottles in return for odd chores I do for them. If you prefer something a little sharper and less sweet, this *johannesbeeren* wine will be perfect with your sandwich. We can drink the mead later, like a dessert."

I tried it—a perfect savoury for the cheese. We relaxed under the apple tree while we ate.

I looked around the garden—saw plantain, calendula, chamomile and asked, "With these plants, the bees, your Aga, the fireplace, mortars and pestles, you wouldn't be making soaps or oils, would you?"

"Yeah, I make a few things. I'm into fragrances. Over there I have stocks and phlox. I've got honeysuckle, wisteria and a patch of regale lilies—even keep some fragrant petunias and tobacco plants."

I was interested in how Bree was growing roots in this Jungfrau Region landscape. It seemed to me that her garden was actually her input (some call it sweat equity, or skin in the game) of her own being into the local landscape—a green bit of psychic recycling—a subtle and not-so-subtle energy flow.

Bree was putting down roots, cultural roots, and inhaling what the local landscape exuded.

Yeah, that's it—plants assist in the development of local cultural roots. And that small-scale effort provides a more detailed and broader understanding/appreciation of the larger landscape.

Thoughts flooded my head—when people move from their birthplace, the place of their youth, they carry with them (within their auras, within their memories) a landscape implant—roots, scents, stories—a very ethereal essence that does not easily disappear—even over a lifetime. I shared these thoughts with Bree and I was intrigued by her response.

"CJ, this is not a new realization. Druidry and permaculture carry, as their base, that very same understanding. If you feel that—we are on the same page."

I nodded my head.

She said, "All those plant and landscape experiences that take you and me to 'the other side', well, that is not new either. Many people call it natural magic. It is there. It is real, and for us Christians, it is a blessing from God. Free for the taking. We have but to humbly open the door."

I was so happy to be hearing that language from Bree. She was, even back in Morocco, a person from the land of Faery.

But my thoughts kept flowing. When human eating and defence depend on local landscape and weather realities, they create definitive values and activities. And the further one moves from that local dependency the less one feels the landscape; but the roots are always there to be prodded by art, music, literature, poetry. It felt so logical.

What gave birth to those thoughts? My easy answer was the Jungfrau Region landscape—not the tourist procession from Interlaken to Jungfraujoch but the perimeter—the part that tourists rarely frequent—like where Bree and I were sitting on the eastern upper edge of the Grindelwald valley.

We talked about all these things. We felt enlivened—like the conversation itself was a very portal.

Bree said, "Portals? Rebirth, renewal, regeneration."

We said no more. We just sat.

The sun traversing the sky moved us out of the shade. Sun was warm, felt healthy. We both enjoyed its warmth. Then we moved our chairs back into the shade. Bree offered me the mead. I drank. Felt good.

She asked, "What are you doing these days, are you an assassin in foreign lands?"

"What?"

"Don't kid me. Back in Morocco, Tangier, weren't you doing stuff with Steve?"

"Steve? What stuff?"

"Steve. The guy everyone called StoneSteve. He helped me on the helicopter after I was kidnapped in the trafficking thing. Steve said you and he were close—colleagues or something—so because of what he was doing I figured you were, how do they say it—in the game."

I laughed, "Really, Bree. I've always been a landscape guy. I did my design study in Tangier and that was it."

"That was it?"

"Well, strange stuff happened. But like you. I had strange stuff done to me; and that is really another story."

"So, you're not an assassin?"

"No, landscape architect. That's what I was doing in Saudi Arabia."

"Okay, so you are not killing people; but you are at the sharp end of capital development and killing the natural landscape, right?"

"Maybe I would say I am taking natural beauty and reorganizing it."

"For what purpose? Look around us here. There are no landscape architects here, nor are they needed."

I said, "Human population growth and the passage of time... changes... somebody has to accommodate those changes... sensibly."

"Sensibly? What does that mean?"

"Since development is inevitable, I try to repair and re-establish the beauty. Hey Bree, like you back in the Peace Corps, I'm just trying to make a difference."

***

Making a Difference

...in CJ's own words...

"Make a difference? Boy, I caught some hell for being a do-gooder back then. Some kind of naive fallacy."

I said, "Do-gooder, I had an explanation from a Hare Krishna person that explained, humans doing good is their nature like the nature of sugar is sweetness. Doing good is our nature. Just have to make use of intelligence to answer the what and how questions."

"That may be well and good, CJ; but let me tell you how I have addressed the 'make a difference' thing."

"Tell me."

"Want me to fill up your mead... this will be a long story?"

"I'm good. I'm seeing primroses, hazelnuts ripening on that red-leaved shrub while watching the sun move across the Grindelwald bowl on its way to sunset. Tell me the story. I'm having a good time today."

Bree began, "It all started just after Morocco. That Sahara desert thing, the West Africa thing and the female trafficking thing had me way off balance. All I knew I had was what I could hear from the landscape."

"Not a small thing, Bree... I've never forgotten what you shared."

"Well, I kept hearing about the alternative types that had been drawn to Glastonbury, so I went—all by myself into that sea of people. That was the first time I met Rastafarians."

189

"Are you into that?"

"Yes and no. Peaceful living with the land, yes. Heavy drug use, no. I like the colours, I like the hair stuff; but that's not the story. While at Glastonbury, I met some Irish ladies. We sat and talked for hours about plants and listening to the landscape. They told me about Beltane. To make a long story short—Beltane's about ages past and how people stayed in touch with the landscape. I can give you more detail if..."

I was casually watching small puffy white clouds form and drift against the mountains only to dissolve and disappear; but I was listening.

I said, "Keep on with the big picture story—the make a difference bit."

"So I kept in touch with those Irish ladies and we arranged to meet up in Interlaken, especially to hear the music of Eluvietie at Greenfields annual music festival—a musical interpretation of Celtic and Gaelic roots.

"A bunch of things happened... came together then for me. Hanging around in groups trying to make things better was too much—too much discussion—too much compromise—too much bullying—too much herd mentality. When I got to Interlaken, I didn't know anything about the landscape; but when I saw the Jungfrau, its magnetism was stronger than Greenfields. I took a train to Grindelwald and started walking up to First, over to Grosse Scheidegg, down to Reichenbach up to Schwarzwaldalp and back to Grindelwald—you know what I found?"

"I can guess; but I'd rather you tell me in your own words."

"The exact opposite of what I found in the Sahara. The Sahara said to me 'get the hell out of here or I'll eat you alive'. The Jungfrau said 'please stay here and love me'."

I could see her heart in her eyes.

She said, "And I've been here ever since."

"We're on the same page... in the same place. But the 'make a difference' stuff?"

***

Paragliding

...in CJ's own words...

"CJ, let me start again with these two words. Hubris. Megalomania. People make mistakes to think they can change anything. I figure, I make my own small life—my food, my shelter right, then everyone I meet can feel my happy vibe. So that's what I am doing. No pretending I am stronger than God, no pretending I am stronger than Gaia. None of that. Simple living, clean living and give an honest smile to everyone I meet."

"You mentioned Gaia—according to the Greeks and feminist environmentalists today, she was worshippable—could that be what we feel in this landscape all about us?"

"I don't really see it that way. This goes back to my times in Glastonbury and at Greenfields in Interlaken. We talked about the Vedic roots, Gayatri—everyone searching. It got weird... golden rule... platinum rule... too much yap-yap!"

"What are you saying?"

"People trying, even arguing to change each other. Life is tough enough by itself. My position on Gaia? Gaia is not the mother of all life but... the Earth, the whole earth, of which we know very little, is, in my opinion, beyond our measuring capacity, beyond our ability to understand... it is the magnificent creation of God."

"Well, we are close. The planet Earth isn't a thing but the home of processes just like our bodies have processes to heal when confronted by danger or attack. I think James Lovelock wrote: Homeostasis by and for the biosphere—I am with that but I differ in that I believe that humans are part and not separate. Humans are part? Definitely—reduction in biodiversity is not a problem but part of a balancing mechanism that we do not yet understand. Humans are not separate from the Earth, they are part of it. They are self-aware and have spiritual enquiring capabilities."

"We are close. I'm tired of all the primordial bullshit speculation! I'm sticking with the ten commandments. And the bottom line for me? There are different levels of life and time that we do not really understand—and we may never—but look at what's all around us... now, today!"

Bree focussed on the local. She brought to my attention the background ringing.

"Ringing?" I asked.

"Don't you find it soothing?"

I listened carefully. I could hear bells ringing, not church bells. With questioning eyes, I looked at Bree. She said, "Listen quietly and carefully. The deeper ringing is from the bells on the cows in pastures nearby. The lighter tingles are from sheep and goats also in nearby pastures. I love the sounds of those bells. These animals enjoy the grasses in these pastures and most of the farmers and their families treat these animals like family members. The ringing bells are peaceful, relaxing. Bells of satisfaction."

I listened. Those bells, like Ed had first mentioned on the train out of Bern, those sweet bells I was now hearing were part of this Jungfrau Region landscape aura. I just listened and relaxed.

Then we were in the sun again. The afternoon warmth healed then the summer temperature broke as it does in the mountains and sunset commenced. We watched the 15-20 paragliders release gracefully as a clustered group from First, each then to slowly find its own way to Grund at the bottom of the Grindelwald bowl. I was reminded of the "seeds of the sacred tree" scene from the movie *Avatar*—fluid, genteel, soft, elegant riding on the wind.

The cool didn't chill, it refreshed; and as the sunset turned into the crepuscule, she asked, "More mead?" Before I could answer she continued, "No, I've got a better idea. How would you like a mug of homemade hot chocolate, *heisse shoggi*, as they call it here. It will keep you warm as the cool mountain air settles in with the night and the stars."

Couldn't say no. But I did say, "How did you know I had a thing for chocolate?" She smiled ever so sweetly. Bree went back inside and a couple minutes later she brought out two mugs of her homemade hot chocolate with spoons.

The chocolate was thick and warm—went right to my core. It was fine. I felt comfortable emotionally—a strange feeling for me—I thought it was something I had missed ever so long. It was the first time I felt a layer of comfort over my worst memories.

We relished the hot chocolate and the changing landscape colours in silence. Then, as the first stars began twinkling, Bree simply said, "Well, CJ, let's go inside and make some new memories."

This time she showed me a small set of stairs in the back corner of her haybarn. The ladder led to the old hay loft. In the roof there were four large skylights that she opened. We could see the glowing, orange-tinted tops of the entire range of Jungfrau Region mountains as the sun dipped in the west.

We took our clothes off, felt the mountains' breezes. And she shook me all night long. She said it, I needed new memories; and at that moment I knew I was in the right place. Healing had finally begun.

The night of hot passion had begun to subside as the sun began to colour the sky. We both felt the chill of the mountain air.

Bree wrapped her arms around me, squeezed tightly then kissed me, whispering, "How about we go downstairs so I can make you another cup of hot chocolate, this time with my special spicing?"

I was floating. I was good.

***

Kurt Says

When I look way back in CJ's diaries and journals to his time in Tangier, I think about cocoons. It all started in Tangier, as far as I am concerned. There was an emotional reality, spoken or not, about cocoons in Tangier.

I put together Sachy, her nickname, Lil' Wing, butterflies and design. They were all swirling about CJ back then. He needed Sachy as his cocoon while he was surrounded by northwest Africa cultural and landscape influences that almost did him in.

But a design cocoon? Design for CJ wasn't a cocoon. Cocoons were his protection from the shocks and dangers life had thrown at him. Design, landscape architecture design was his blood.

And on the subject of Sachy and their kids, CJ was finally rescued, re-birthed emotionally by Bree. With Bree, a new life opened for him. This was another obvious reason I had to rule out suicide in Cairo.

Like I said earlier, I can't understand why he left the Jungfrau Region. I knew he liked projects; but everything had lined up for him in the Grindelwald area. There are a lot of unanswered questions. I had no evidence yet.

I wonder if Bree is in the picture—does she know about CJ's official death? Maybe I should try to contact her... she lives isolated in a haybarn... maybe Suzie at the Blumisalp Stubbe... no, they weren't on good terms... no way I was going to butt in. And hell, I didn't even know myself for sure if CJ was dead.

***

Jobs is on the Way

...in CJ's own words...

I woke up with a clear head. My focus was Bree. It was more than physical. I felt like I had had a thorough internal cleansing. The decade-old memory of the horrific deaths of Sachy and our kids had metastasized into a huge emotional boil that I had held inside. Bree had lanced it and begun healing the wound. That meant something special to me.

With that same clarity, I realized that my time with Bree had been at the expense of my hotel room. I told Bree the same. She said, "Why stay in a hotel? What's your plan, your schedule? If you have nothing to do, stay with me... my garden always accepts extra care."

We walked outside into her garden where she immediately started tending to the plants. The weather was clear and calm—another beautiful day. My head was going fast. Up until now, I figured my most important task was to get another job—no income. Bree had offered me a full-service place to stay and time with her in her wonderful garden in the Grindelwaldtal. Maybe too much had happened too fast.

"Let me go and get my things. I need to check to see if I have any job offers and up here we have no Internet connectivity. If I head down into town now, I should be back with my stuff in early afternoon."

I had been away from my hotel for two days. Heading back, I walked downhill using the Grindelwald church steeple to guide my general direction.

I looked back over my shoulder a couple times; and Bree was always there waving to me. I wondered where was I going with her? This had been very special. She made the connection between the small-scale and the large-scale transcendencies— who else? Nobody. She was special. But I had seen her only twice in 20 years...

Getting back into Grindelwald took me about 30 minutes of steady downhill walking. Returning to the hotel, I was met at the front desk by questions. Was I alright? Did I need any assistance? I assured them all was well; but inside I had a strange feeling that maybe Bree was my future.

Back in my room the first thing I did was go out on the balcony. Standing on the balcony, I swept my eyes up and down, left and right across the Shreckhorn and the Eiger.

Where had I just been? Bree? One-night stand? No, she helped me step forward with my life. She was an emotional healer. And she was a landscape person... still that way after 20 years. I forced my eyes off the steep, rich, mountain landscape, turned around and went back inside. I began to check my email.

An email from my old boss, Will in Yenbo, read:

Re-assessment of Yenbo program schedule has been delayed and still uncertain.

A position has opened in Cairo, Egypt. We have an urgent requirement to manage the front-end study for a new town of 75,000 people, just outside of Cairo.

This would be an extendable fifteen-month contract assignment. We need someone on the ground there and on the job in two weeks at the latest.

We will provide business class tickets, fifteen months' residence, room and board in the Mena House Oberoi and standard expatriate bachelor package. Your colleague, Alan, from Yenbo and Riyadh is already on the ground and overseeing the definition of the scope of work. He too is installed in Mena House and you should contact and collaborate with him as soon as you arrive.

This opportunity can be yours. Email immediately if you are interested.

I re-read the email three times. I read it again, a fourth time. A job offer. Fifteen months in Cairo, Egypt. I felt stirred. I felt as if some big puzzle pieces that hadn't been fitting in had just nicely found their place.

But Alan again? He had been a problem in Yenbo. I emailed my concern to Will. He answered back immediately saying this was not the time to take issue. I thought for about two minutes. Then I emailed back.

Definitely interested. Available immediately. Please send details.

My mind was already on the job—Umm Kalthum, *Descent into Egypt*—all seemed to be coming together. And I was planning my trip to Amsterdam to prepare for my Cairo departure and also to visit my old haunts, the bookstores, the coffee shops, the brown cafes, the gardens, the museums—I really missed the Stedelijk and my old favourite, Landloper Cafe. I fell right back into my old routine, the work cocoon I had built over my six years in Yenbo and even before in LA... but... Bree... overwhelmed those shallow past priorities.

It hadn't taken much for my mind to start racing into landscape design. Shallow? Do-gooder? My design cocoon wove quickly—Cairo, music, Sahara landscape—what might I find? Design thoughts once again filled my head. The Jungfrau Region landscape had reignited my thoughts of transcendent design. And Cairo fired my interests in my travel/foreign culture experiences... I had always seen design built on a concept from observation of local natural and social landscape realities. And my discussions with Bree had not changed that.

From local landscape observations, I physically, emotionally and intellectually linked my selection of the plants, the paving, the water and all other physical design components. I was full-blown into my design cocoon. My Moroccan experiences had taken me a step beyond—into an arcane territory—that could carry the user to blissful enjoyment. But the practical world of clients and regulations tempered my hopes for transcendent design. Bree and the Jungfrau Region had once again awakened my transcendent landscape feelings but also tempered them with reality. What would Cairo hold?

I went through all the train and hotel booking details for setting up my trip to Amsterdam.

I was presented a door and I walked through it. Alive, I felt alive in a world I knew!

A new email arrived from my old boss with confirmed details for my new job. By early afternoon, the job agreement was finalized. Travel arrangements, hotel and everything to Amsterdam were completed. Packing was no big deal. Before beginning my quest for Kaytee, I had already shipped my personal effects from Yenbo to temporary storage in Amsterdam.

I picked up the Algernon Blackwood book from my bed table and opened it again to the table of contents. I was about to make my own "Descent into Egypt". Blackwood had, like me, been inspired by the forest trees in the Swiss landscape. And I recalled the mesmerizing music of that Egyptian lady from the countryside, Umm Kalthum. Another wave of excitement. Then a wave of uncertainty. I couldn't really tell them apart. But the whole mix of a new job and a move to Cairo had flipped a switch for me. The old days were alive and well... but... Bree... there was no way to contact her about my new job.

I had to see her. I had to go over everything with her. There were two things here in Grindelwald that totally overwhelmed me, the landscape and Bree—both were strong and sweet. I packed up my stuff, ready to leave for Amsterdam. I had told Bree I would be back but this job... it got in the way. I had no way to contact her other than walking back to her haybarn. I'd do that in the morning. Then I took rest for my last night in Grindelwald.

***

Kurt Says

A ha! Another clue! CJ must work in Cairo with an already out-of-favour colleague. So, all was probably not so glorious in Cairo. And it is an on-going what I call "CIA" thread, active with CJ in Cairo.

I was surprised also that the new job put his time with Bree in the background. That said, I always knew CJ to dig into his work. He loved landscape architecture projects. And CJ's penchant for design was still alive and strong. Maybe I'll get something out of his design musings after all. But his death... still a mystery.

I tried to contact his employer and his boss Will Clendenon over the phone and in person at their LA headquarters—they treated me like an unauthorized reporter or gumshoe investigator. They confirmed that CJ had died in Cairo—and I got nothing more from them.

So I had nothing new about CJ in Cairo. I was convinced it wasn't suicide; but what happened? Murder? What was CJ into that I couldn't make out from his writings?

He had everything to live for—Bree, his design explorations, a good job. Murdered or walking about off the grid. If I had to choose? Walkabout. I need some evidence. And frankly, after weeks of going through CJ's writings—I've got nothing. Nothing clear about his fate in Cairo. And nothing final from his landscape design quest. Nothing.

***

Goodbyes

...in CJ's own words...

I stored my things with the kept luggage at the hotel. Then, even before breakfast, I took off up the slope toward Grosse Scheidegg. I followed the path from the other night like a hound dog. I arrived at Bree's before 8, knocked and she answered.

She said, "And when do you leave?"

"How did you know?"

She said nothing but the sadness in her eyes told me everything.

"Listen," I said, "I'm going to Cairo for a 15-month job. And I will be back here in 6 months. We can have a real talk then. In the meantime, I've got to practise my trade, my profession."

She said, "Cairo? Egypt? The Sahara? Really! Twenty years ago the Sahara was mean, intolerable, filled with an angry vibe that drove me out—you forget?"

"No, not at all. But work is work."

Silence in the morning mountain sun. I struggled to say, "I feel a bond with you... that makes it ever so hard to say goodbye. A seed may have been planted twenty years ago and it might have just germinated. I don't want it to wither, do you follow?"

I tried to stay detached but something in my heart let those words flow.

She looked at me. Our eyes locked.

She said, "So be it. I will always be here. I love this place; and with you I have been satisfied as never before. You know what that means?"

I looked deep into her eyes. She received me.

She said, "I owe you and you are welcome anytime. Now get out of here before I lock you down."

I wheeled and left immediately downhill. The emotions that turn to tears were building up. I kept walking fast. Finally, after a respectful distance, I stopped and looked back. She was there, waving. I waved back.

I had to hustle back to town to make the schedule work.

Back in Grindelwald, I picked up my gear and headed over to the stubbe. I had given a lot of thought to my time with Suzie and her steady helpfulness. Suzie and I had shared some landscape things... deep. But that was all eclipsed by my time with Bree. I concluded I had to move forward with my new project and my refreshed design quest, focussing on music.

At the stubbe, I said, "Hi Suzie, how're you doing?"

She looked at me, paused for a moment, looking me up and down again, then asked, "I'm fine, *mais comment vas-tu?* You're looking energized today, what's going on?"

"I'm feeling great. Had a long night sleep. Definitely refreshed. And I don't know where to start with thank yous... now let me return this Blackwood book to you—really eye-opening stuff it is. This guy might be the best landscape writer I've ever read. It was great—his *Descent into Egypt* really got me."

"If you like it, take it with you."

"Really? Thank you. But I've got more to tell. News! Of all things, you can't guess what happened yesterday. I've been offered and taken a job in Cairo. Can you believe that? It's all come together in the last twelve hours. So that book will definitely come in handy."

Her barkeep instincts gave her separation as she listened.

"I have a fifteen-month assignment in Giza, right next to the Sphinx and Pyramids."

"*Magnifique!* You must be happy! You look it, that's for sure!"

"Yeah, I didn't know how much I was missing work, as if half of me was empty and now it's full. I have to flow with this one. I'm taking the train this afternoon to Zurich, then direct to

Amsterdam where I'll get my personal things in order for the flight to Cairo in a week."

"Amsterdam? What's up with that?"

"It is my path to Cairo. I've business to take care of and, yeah, I know my way around there. Been taking vacations there regularly for the past six years. My week up there'll give me time to prepare for the trip and let these intense days in Grindelwald find their own level inside me. My thoughts, emotions, intellect, my bodily core have all been stirred here. I have only you to thank for all that."

I got Suzie's email address and thanked her for all the people she had introduced. I asked her to remember me to them when they next came in, Ian, Peter, especially LN... I paused for an unconscious moment... then my eyes focussed out the window at the Shreckhorn and the Unterergletscher. My higher instincts—motivations took over. Then I shook my head, looked back at Suzie, said my last goodbyes, hugged her in European-goodbye-fashion and rushed to the train station.

Before I climbed onto the train out of Grindelwald, I looked one last time at the panorama of Wetterhorn, Shreckhorn, Eiger, and their massive landscape dominance. I looked at the little village around me, and then at the farmer chalets and their haybarns tucked in naturally at the distant foot of the mountain forests. I looked at the patchwork of rich, floriferous pastures.

I took in a deep breath.

I held it.

I released it.

Then I smiled and climbed onto the train.

6-Kurt In Cairo

Ahlan wa Sahlan

...from Kurt again...

I had put my office duties on the back burner while spending weeks reviewing CJ's diaries and design journals, patching together CJ's pilgrimages to and from KSA.

I know he was on to something as he headed to Cairo. It was a design something, he had called it effulgent design. In my opinion it still needed refining. It needed street cred. It had to be practical. But I had nothing useful.

Cairo, for my searching, had remained a dead end. I had no evidence, no writings from CJ in Cairo. But what happened in Cairo?? Murder or something else? There was something odd. Something didn't sit right. I finally had to set everything aside and get back into my daily life, my normal life, the office.

I had just about put CJ out of my mind... almost a year had passed. And can you believe it?!

I heard from Cal, that old bud of mine, working in Cairo. I had tried to contact him a couple times after I had come home from Amsterdam. He never answered. So, I was surprised. What a bomb!

Cal, an old high school friend, a surfing bud, had been for more than a decade a librarian and teacher at Cairo American College. He was now working in Cairo as an archivist, somehow a part of the US Embassy staff. In an email, he wrote:

Kurt,

If you ever have one of your international design conferences in
Cairo let me know, because, a while ago, remember when you
asked about the death of your colleague, Christopher Janus.
Well, it has just come to my attention that indeed there was a
package of his personal effects collected from his vehicle.

I could arrange to have you view them. Let me know if this is of
any use.

Cal

I emailed back, No way!

Cal responded, Way!

So it was on. Cairo has always been one of those "can't miss"
places. World history demands it. Hell, the movies demand
it. I saw at the Getty one time, images of old Cairo that were
part of David Roberts' Egyptian art. I was ready; but nervous.
International travels were never my thing.

I was still hungry for answers. What had Cal found for me?
I asked him but he said all was confidential and he assured me
I would find much of it helpful.

So I decided I must go to Cairo. To prepare, rather than
using Wikipedia, I read every novel and watched every movie
about Egyptian "Mummies". It was fun reading—a real blast;
but... was any of it the truth? I even read Blackwood's *Descent
into Egypt*—that was weird about the desert transforming
people from real life into the ancient past—didn't know what
to make of it. Maybe CJ took it seriously... and if so? What? I
was searching for truth. I held tightly to grains of hope. When
I was as ready as I could be, off I went for a planned ten days
in Cairo.

I flew direct LA:Cairo. The Cairo International Airport
serves 20 million residents. I should have figured. I'd been
spoiled last year by the luxury wedding cake that is Dubai
International Airport. Dubai and Cairo are not the same.
I arrived in an airport that was like a huge, overpopulated
market, might as well been the 1930s. No air conditioning and
the crowd was intolerably intense. Couldn't find my bud Cal.

After 30 minutes of fending off hordes of what? Taxi drivers? I grabbed my mobile to call him.

"Hey, what's up? I'm out of it. Where are you? I've looked everywhere for you."

Cal said, "I hear you. Listen, I'm tied up at the office. Glad you made it. I'll send one of our drivers. Houssam will have a sign with your name 'Kurt' on it and meet you just outside the door after you exit from customs, okay?"

"How long?"

"Takes about 30 minutes without traffic. Call me back if the rendezvous doesn't work. You good to go?"

"I'm reading you."

But I wasn't convinced. I backtracked to the exit from customs and waited. And waited. At only 10AM, the weather was unbearably hot and sticky outside. I was swooning in the heat; this wasn't the Med climate I knew from LA. On top of that, every time I stepped outside—big time—shooing off flies and more taxi guys, both in numbers and equally irritating. I tried to find some place cool and quiet.

After about 45 minutes I saw a guy holding an 11x17 size whiteboard with my name, Kurt. I was disappointed he was not wearing a red Fez hat. He looked the type.

Big guy and an even bigger friendly smile. Reached out, grabbed my hand and shook it saying, "*Ahlan wa sahlan*, welcome to Cairo. I'm Houssam, follow me quickly, I'm in a no-parking zone."

***

Houssam

I grabbed my wheelie and followed. He opened the backseat door of a dusty and dirty 1970s, 7-Series BMW, black with shaded windows.

"*Fadlak*, please put your stuff in the back and hop into the front seat."

I did. I asked, "Who are all those guys around here? Are they all taxi drivers?"

"Yes and no—it's complicated. We just call them dragomen." Then he closed the trunk and motioned me to the passenger side front door.

As soon as he got in and turned the key, the sound system thumped a bouncing deep base Arabic hip hop.

He asked, "Do you know Ashekman?"

"What? Can't hear you."

He turned down the sound.

"Ashekman—Beirut hip hop."

"Oh?"

"*Ya Reit*," he said without stopping, "that's the name of this one—*ya reit* means I wish in Arabic, the song lyrics are all about being go-getters vs passive in life—it's about seizing every opportunity and never having to say I wish I had done it."

He turned it up.

I said, "Hot in the car."

"Sorry *ma'fi*, AC—kaput." He opened the windows and turned the hip hop louder. Car was rocking—nothing wrong with the sound system.

Houssam drove that BMW like a pile driver on steroids.

"We'll take the by-pass—it's limited access—we'll get there faster." It was always foot on the gas, hand on the horn—all speed, all noise. Too much for me. This was why I didn't travel much.

He volunteered, "It's the only way to drive in Cairo. Been here eight years. Did university here. Love this place. Born in Lebanon. Hey, this driving bother you? I heard you been to Dubai."

"Dubai? Yeah, but this isn't how they drove in Dubai. If I remember, people kept in their lanes—except for Royal Family and their close friends. They always drove the shoulders at twice the speed limit. But here—those left-turn/U-turn lanes—never seen anything like it."

Houssam said, "If I waited in those long lines, I'd never get anything done."

I can't count how many times I had to grit my teeth as Houssam pile drove his way through Cairo over the next half hour.

Left turns? Not at intersections but about 500 meters after the overpass intersections, there were long double left turn and U-turn only lanes, always bumper to bumper crawling both lanes, 40-50 cars backed up in each lane then a third lane of cars trying to cut in out of the fast lane.

But Houssam had his technique. He sped past all three lines and hit the brakes hard and swerved into the very head of the line, hardly slowing down as he wedged around everyone else and completed his U-turn in less time than it takes to puff once on a cigarette. It always looked like an imminent sideswipe and rear-ender at the same time.

Good thing I hadn't eaten the usual three meals on the long international flight. Would have been blown all over the car. One time he emergency braked, screeching and handbrake turning. Never saw anything like it.

I asked, "Police ever stop you?"

"Police? Never."

We crossed the heart of the city and, before a half hour, were on the west side of Cairo. I just had a trip from the Sinai desert to Giza. When I first saw it, the Great Pyramid on the western horizon caused me a strange and awkwardly overwhelming tingle.

Up till now Houssam's driving had captured all my attention. But now, I wondered about the guys who built the pyramids... would they drive like Houssam if they were alive today? Intensity. Such is Cairo.

We arrived without further incident at the rear entry to the US Embassy.

***

Archive

...Kurt continues...

Under the watchful eye of a US Marine guard, Cal met me outside the building. Houssam, job finished, left to park his car. Cal and I exchanged greetings—old friends from California. He warned me that as soon as we entered the embassy, the Marine thorough check-in procedure would take some time. US Embassy security was a serious thing—his exact words.

Finally, after an arduous check-in procedure, where they disassembled and I reassembled my MacBook Pro, Cal took me downstairs into a private reading room.

He brought in an A4 sized locked metal box. He unlocked it, telling me the contents were confiscated from Janus' rental car the day after the accident. Then, as he prepared to leave the room, he told me I had one hour to do whatever I liked; but all items had to be returned to the box exactly as I found them.

When I examined the contents of the box, I found a folder, with a handwritten label—Janus' Records, his US passport number and Social Security number. Inside the folder was an inventory of everything of CJ's in the metal box—only two items. The two items were a boxed set of CDs and a thumb drive. Okay, now I was into it. I thirsted for truth—for answers to CJ's mystery. Finally. Nervous. Excited.

The boxed set was Scriabin music CDs, containing four discs. I wondered, who the hell is Scriabin. The thumb drive intrigued me more.

But when I opened the boxed set, I found, slipped in, a couple pieces of paper, three items to be exact. One was a withdrawal receipt from the Cairo Citi-Bank for US$3,000, dated two years ago. Was that a useful clue? Originally, I had seen that withdrawal with the Amsterdam bankers. I checked my timeline and noted it occurred just about six months before he was declared dead. I thought. It made sense if he was paying someone off for something or... if he was going on walkabout. It was easy for me to conclude the latter.

The remaining two pieces of paper had CJ's handwriting. One piece had both the Latin and English texts of Gregorio Allegri's *Miserere mei Deus.* On the second piece was written a list of Egyptian geography or tourist destinations including: Thebes, Memnon, Helwan, Abu Simbal. No notes, just a list. Interesting but I held hope for the thumb drive.

I plugged it in. Mounted without problem. Two gigs— contained two files, each in PDF format. The first file was Arthur Conan Doyle's short story, entitled, *The Tragedy of the Korosko.* The second file was a book by Virginia Danielson, entitled *The Voice of Egypt: Umm Kulthum, Arabic Song, and Egyptian Society in the Twentieth Century.* Well, CJ was into literature and music— he had spoken of Umm Kulthum—maybe this was about his landscape and music design explorations. I hoped CJ had made some notes.

I played the Scriabin CDs as I worked. They were weird, big-time weird. I got no inspiration—I didn't like them at all. I wondered what CJ heard or found in them.

On my MacBook, I made digital copies of everything. Something was not right. It was a sad feeling I had as I looked at these paltry remnants from CJ's Cairo. He was chasing something. And when he was in the hunt, he wouldn't stop. I turned over and over the contents. They defied easy answers. I sensed a melancholy sadness, somewhere near, a tragedy. The opposite of the tingle I felt when I first saw the Great Pyramid. Cairo had become a city, a place of feelings. This wasn't my normal. I kept searching. I wasn't satisfied that what I had just seen had any useful information.

CJ's records, the ones I got originally from Amsterdam,

stopped the day he left Grindelwald. Even with these new things from Cairo, there were no new design journals, no diaries. No entries, no notes from CJ's time spent in Amsterdam and Cairo two years ago. CJ was always disciplined in keeping these records. But they were mysteriously absent over those twelve months between his departure from Grindelwald and his "death" in Cairo. So, I did not have the benefit of his first-person thoughts, observations and conclusions.

For me, this story was all about the life and death intrigue of my friend. But secondarily I had become enthralled by his, a landscape architect's, quest for design with meaning.

The personal items collected from CJ's abandoned rental car, those artefacts, clearly showed he was doggedly following a path on which he had already made distinct progress while in Switzerland—music and the landscape. Even though my first review of the PDFs was cursory, each item covered issues in the forefront of CJ's earlier design efforts. I recalled what had been the memorable topics from his design journals. Cultures. Plants. Gardens. Landscapes. Music. Beauty. Paths. Journeys. Layers. Windows. Threads. Skeins.

Skeins? That was CJ's word. A word I as a landscape architect had never heard, in school or practice. Of all these issues that CJ liked, it was skeins that caught me. He described a skein as something emanating from plants. CJ guessed that skeins grounded a person. He called them real cultural linkages.

He went further, suggesting that skeins also provided an aura that could bring to garden visitors the access to transcendent ecstasy. His explanations were beyond me. But he had a way to take something complex and make it simple. And me, I was still hoping to plug into his energy and grow my firm's reputation. His life energy was strong. I was intrigued. I had been hooked.

He couldn't be dead. That kept returning to my thoughts.

One thing became clear to me. CJ was entranced with Egypt. He had dug right in. I asked myself why?

Then I heard the door open. It was Cal.

I immediately thanked him, "Dude, you're a rockstar!"

He asked, "Did you find anything useful?"

"Your help has been useful. And it was a blast going through his stuff. But, useful? Is a mystery useful?"

"How's that? Tell me. Take it from the top."

"My colleague was onto something but I'm not sure what he was doing. I need some more time. He has been on some kind of quest; and I am hoping that if I can put the pieces together I may understand two things. First and foremost his 'death'. Second, maybe he might have found some design seeds of change—if not an actual reveal of the design force he argued landscape architecture had been missing."

Cal said, "I don't know about that design stuff; but you have seen everything available. Sounds like what you read might be helpful."

"Have you showed me everything? Everything? If so, I need more time."

Cal looked strangely at me as if I questioned his manhood, then he said, "I've given everything I found. You mean you need more time? Are we on the same wavelength?"

"I need to examine everything more closely. I didn't come all the way from LA to go home with doubts. I am hoping to solve a strange mystery that has to do with CJ's six years in Saudi Arabia; and it all ends here in Cairo."

"So, how can I help any further?"

"Cal, you're the upmost. You've given me real leads. Until now, I've been in the dark for too long on this. Do you read me? Here's what I'd like to do. I want to stay longer in Cairo and closer to where his car was found near the Pyramids. In fact, I'd like to go to the Pyramids. They are a strange presence... when your driver, Houssam brought me across town, the first time I saw them... on the western horizon... I felt a tingle on my spine. We seen some monster waves but this was different."

"You sure it wasn't Houssam's ride?"

"That too; but the massive pyramids, after thousands of years... plucked some kind of chord. Something inside, deep. I'd call it a tingle but it was more like a deep rumble. Uneasiness all over me."

"Are you for real? Heavy. What exactly do you want to do?"

"I've copied CJ's records onto my MacBook. I'd like to spend a few days going through them... around the pyramids. Are you down with that? After all, that is where his abandoned car was found, right?"

"You're right, bro. Maybe I can help you. We keep a couple rooms on reserve at the Mina House—it's directly in front of the Great Pyramid of Giza. Would you like to stay there? I can make arrangements. You'll just have to reimburse us the base daily rate."

"Epic. Yeah, I like the sound of that. I need to adjust my previous reservations from a hotel on the Nile. Can I borrow Houssam for that?"

"I'm reading you just fine, no sweat, let me make a couple phone calls and then Houssam can take you to your Nile hotel and then to the Mina House. The hotel also organizes dependable visits to the pyramids that include going inside."

Sounded good to me.

***

Giza

I checked in to the Mina House. My room was in a garden wing. No view of the Pyramids. I crashed. Jet lag, or something, knocked me out.

When I woke it was almost dark. Showered, dressed and after consulting the hotel brochure, went over to the in-house Sultan Lounge which had a beautiful terrace garden facing the Great Pyramid. I thought it would be a safe place to get my first close-up look at that 5,000-year-old landmark.

They had powerful lights on its face. I was fascinated by the peak against the last of sunset. As the sky turned into nighttime black, the rising moon sliver appeared. I got my money's worth—strange combination of airiness and gravitas. I not only saw, but felt the beauty that made life worth living. A world wonder—definitely. Far out! I couldn't stop staring.

The longer I fixated on the pyramid, the further receded the airiness of the moon and began inside me something uncomfortable... a danger, a warning. This place was strange. What happened to CJ? Needed to focus my thoughts.

I opened my TextEdit of notes from CJ's writings and did a couple searches. I found one clue that I hadn't seen before. CJ had mentioned a great-uncle from his mother's side, Patrick Moleson, who had spent time in Egypt.

I went online and discovered his great-uncle was actually an Egyptologist. Patrick Moleson had spent years in Thebes and every place else between there and Cairo. He had written

216

a book, *A Modern Reconstruction of Sun-worship in Ancient Egypt*. The life source, he speculated, was heat, heat from the sun.

I dug deeper... why? I don't know... maybe I'd find a crumb, a clue... something to grab onto, something that might lead me to CJ, to the truth of his time in Egypt. What I found was weird. The only record of Patrick Moleson was in the details of *Descent into Egypt* by Algernon Blackwood. I'd read that when I was preparing for coming here. Didn't know what to make of it then... and now? Maybe something I could get into. Mysteries everywhere I turned.

The next day I decided to get into the real thing. With the hotel's assistance, I arranged a private guide to take me around and into the Great Pyramid. The guide walked me past hundreds of dragomen—more than the airport. Legions of camels and camel jockeys. And thousands of tourists.

The scale of the pyramid—immense. Humbling. But it was the trip inside that blew me away me. Damp, dark—the humidity of thousands of years without sunlight. A strange kind of strangling—it suffocated. Tried to tolerate but the effect on my lungs transferred to my brain, which no longer was able to analyze that which was input through my senses. My legs failed. The guide led me by hand and my thoughts went dark until we re-emerged into the glare of Egyptian summer high noon. Wipeout.

I couldn't wait to get back to my room. AC. I put the window shades down to protect me from the sun's oppressive glare. Hit the showers. Cold this time. Flushed out my nose, my mouth, my throat. Did some deep breathing. Gradually worked up the shower temp to hot. Deep cleaning. Lay down on the bed and relaxed. Assessed what had just happened. The power. The intensity. What the hell was CJ into? Had he felt this?

This was all getting too deep. I needed to narrow my focus to something real. I fired up my computer to explore in detail the Cairo records that Cal had found for me. The Cairo records had to have a clue. Each item of his record, each artifact was rich in context and the largest context was the landscape. What was CJ finding in this Egyptian landscape? Some design insight? That's what I hoped. But what happened to him?

His Cairo records were four:
1. Allegri's Miserere;
2. Scriabin's music;
3. Doyle's story of the Korosko; and,
4. Danielson's study of Umm Kulthum.

Here is how I interpreted their value. I had two criteria: what happened to CJ and was there any design insight I could use back in LA.

Allegri's Miserere

This was the only clue that I could tie to Amsterdam. On research, I found that during CJ's last stay in Amsterdam, the Concertgebouw hosted a series of performances by Harry Christopher's group, The Sixteen. They performed a number of different versions of Gregorio Allegri's *Miserere mei.*

Miserere tells a sombre story of humans along with the importance of humility and spiritual knowledge as exemplified by the presence and absence of light—during the darkest hours of uncertainty, of the night just before dawn following the crucifixion of Jesus Christ. I can only speculate that CJ, while in Amsterdam, attended the performance of this piece at the Concertgebouw. Maybe he found it instructive to build, with positive certainty, his spiritual and design unity. Nothing that I could drop in on.

I found a version on YouTube and listening to Allegri's Miserere, I felt such an intense sadness, a sweet sadness that overflowed my heart with thoughts of CJ's unceasing struggle with the internal noise—the inner landscape—the uncertainties of life.

This was more about CJ's personal life

Scriabin

I did some research on the composer Scriabin—a weird duck—off the deep end as far as I am concerned. But CJ's choice of Scriabin showed the breadth of his own long-term seeking to learn the history of human search for linking spirit with beauty, life and music. That was CJ all over—how to connect the natural and the spiritual. He regularly asked the question how the gross senses can transform sensual portals via subtle access to ecstatic transcendence. I think that was Scriabin's gig too.

And what did Scriabin have to do with Egypt? He searched for and developed a universal chord. He called it a mystic chord—a chord that transcended all music, a chord that could transcendentally link with ancient civilizations—a chord comprised of the totality of divine powers, designed to afford instant apprehension of... that is, to reveal... what was, in essence, beyond the mind of man to conceptualize. That's some heavy shit—but that is what CJ got into.

Scriabin was a man who by smell, hearing and sight attempted to lead humans to some sort of portal, similar to the efforts by CJ. Unfortunately, I found, with my Google searches on Scriabin, that CJ may have found a darker side. I do hope this was not part of the mystery of his disappearance and apparent death. I do hope this was not an addition to the internal noise he was trying to dissipate.

I had gotten so deep into CJ's design thoughts that I was almost as dizzy reading them as I was inside the pyramid. CJ and design? I always said "over the top". But my experience inside the pyramid dwarfed "over the top". Scriabin? Nothing to see here.

Korosko

This clue, courtesy of Arthur Conan Doyle, showed CJ's continuing respect for books. Perhaps it exemplifies CJ's quest for landscape and garden doors to the transcendent. But me, I'm more pragmatic. I think he tried to gain perspective on the religious or cultural ambiguities he confronted in Cairo. Only my guesswork. CJ made no notes.

Umm Kulthum

CJ had on the thumb drive Virginia Danielson's entire volume, *The Voice of Egypt: Umm Kulthum, Arabic Song, and Egyptian Society in the Twentieth Century*, published in 1997 by The American University in Cairo Press. I did my research. Virginia Danielson was curator of the Archive of World Music and keeper of the Isham Memorial Library at Harvard University. She spent six years in Egypt assembling this academic volume. She was a respectable source.

I read the abstract, the introduction and the summary. Umm Kulthum brought her sensitivities for the rural landscape and its people from her childhood into her music, which reminded urban dwellers everywhere that they still had roots in the country landscape. Her work sprang from her rural roots, people of the landscape, and provided them musical portals that freed them from time and space.

This obviously attracted CJ. I'm pretty clear about that. I can only speculate that CJ may have discovered, in Umm Kulthum, some kind of landscape-related threads, connections with music that enlarged his recent realizations regarding yodelling in Grindelwald. This is where I hoped CJ might have shared a design discovery—but for me? No man's land.

Conclusion

CJ was strong but he carried a huge amount of hurt. Hurt he was trying to work through. He used his design quest two ways. First it served as a kind of emotional shelter. But more important, his design quest was CJ's active well of hope. He was hoping. He was searching. And I? I still had nothing.

***

M'asalaama Cairo

...Kurt continues...

I had resigned myself. My trip to Cairo—fruitless. No new CJ info, no new CJ design insights.

I was in the hotel preparing to return to the US. My flight out of Cairo was that evening, when I received a call from the front desk informing me that someone was hand-delivering a package to me and needed to see me receive it in my hand.

What was this all about? I had already said goodbye to my friend at the US Embassy. I was not expecting anything. I immediately went down to the front desk. The clerk pointed me toward a lady who was also at the front desk.

I paused for a minute to look at her. Who was that stray cat? She looked 40-ish, carried a black sport bag over her shoulder. The sport bag had a huge brass padlock. She was tall, pushing six feet. She was lithe, not anorexic, but in good shape. She had short brown hair, not styled, not fashionable, but work-like. She was attractive in her efficient way. She certainly did not look like a tourist or a businessperson. She wore a long blue cowboy shirt—looked like a Texan. I could see her in any "country and western" bar or movie set.

Before I was ready, she stepped over to me and asked, "Kurt? CJ's colleague?"

I nodded.

Then she handed me a thick 9x12inch sealed and unlabelled manila envelope saying, "Please read everything carefully. I am just a messenger." Before I could even react, she had turned and left the hotel.

On the day, I was confused. I had just finished packing to catch my evening flight back to the US. I was worried as always about an international flight. This envelope thing was extra baggage, or so I thought. I had to finish my preparations for leaving the hotel, so I took the envelope back to my room before opening it. I didn't want another Egyptian mystery.

The package had an inch thick stack of 8.5x11 papers held at the top left by one of those big heavy duty spring paper clamps. The entire package looked and felt like American style.

The top sheet was blank. The second sheet caught my attention. It was a cover note in the style of a 1970s kidnapper ransom note fashioned from individual letters cut out from the English text found in local newspapers and glued on a blank sheet of paper. The note said:

> I have known CJ longer than you. I am certain he has not died. More I cannot tell you. I hope you find the copy of his last design journal useful; but keep it private for the next ten years, or you may likely endanger your own professional career.

I thought... what?!!

The rest of the sheets, maybe 50 of them, were old-style zerox copies. They were copies of what appeared to be the last six months of CJ's diaries and design journals covering his time from Grindelwald to Amsterdam and his first twelve months in Cairo. Some partial and some entire pages in the Zerox had been blacked out.

I read it all in my room and later, multiple times during my flight home. Now, let me get to the point. Generally, with some exceptions, these new pages confirmed my assumptions listed earlier from my visit to the local US Embassy. Though still without proof I am 99% convinced he is on walkabout. He had nothing new design-wise. He was still on the hunt.

The exceptions were important because they gave his design quest a stronger focus, especially in regard to the Egyptian landscape. In these new entries, CJ placed extensive analysis and emphasis on Blackwood's *Descent into Egypt* as an in-depth study of landscape, with focus on its cultural and social components. Blackwood clearly believed, or hoped, that the mysteries of ancient Egypt were indeed still accessible in the landscape. CJ was hunting for that "feeling", he called it transcendent, a most remarkable feeling, for it included yearning. The yearning, to paraphrase Blackwood, for some nameless, forgotten loveliness the world had lost. I wondered if this was what CJ was searching for. But is he alive or dead? All this travel and no certainty. I can only guess.

CJ further speculated that the incredible popularity of Umm Kulthum and her country roots derived from blood in her arteries that came directly from the deep Egyptian landscape. What about CJ's design quest? He was obviously still on that trail.

So, is this the end? What happened to CJ? He was, dare I say, he appeared to be obsessed with Blackwood's *Descent into Egypt*. I had read the story before. I had the pdf on my computer. Re-read it a couple times on the way home. The story had a bright side and a dark side. It also had a music facet that tied to some kind of glorious beauty.

I could understand CJ's interest; but if he was not dead, where was he? Anywhere? Walkabout? A shadow of his former self? Another Egyptian mystery? Was this just another approach to transfiguration, to transcendent effulgences?

Or, did Pharaohs have landscape architects?

***

Hitting the Surf

...Kurt continues...

Funny thing though as I reviewed all CJ's documents, I realized I had gotten closer to him after he left LA than when we worked together. He was hunting for something. What was it, the holy grail? I didn't know. Nevertheless, even without knowing the ultimate goal, at times I greatly enjoyed vicarious pleasure from his quest. His journey was fascinating, full of design breadcrumbs and outright inspiration.

A career cut too short. He was hot on the hunt. His design journals were breadcrumbs; but... there was something unsaid, undone. Still I followed. I could only imagine his experiences and his... unknowns. And when I did I shuddered... like never before.

Shuddered? I was reading a novel, CJ's novel—was it a quest? A mystery? And what about that "CIA" thread? Disappeared? What was that all about? Maybe nothing. I was a SoCal landscape architect and, aside from the surf, my business was my life.

But honestly, as excited as I was about some of his design writings, I would never even try to sell something like effulgent design or transcendent design to any client or architect. Enough is enough.

If that lady at my Cairo hotel was convinced CJ was alive and went to the trouble to tell me... then CJ must be alive. That fit the feelings and conclusions I gathered from CJ's own writing.

But if CJ's still alive—why is everyone else, the Amsterdam

bank people, his company, etc. saying he is dead? I'm frustrated. Despite the note from that Texas cowgirl, I still don't know for sure that CJ is alive—or dead. I am tired of these unanswered questions. Too tired!

CJ might just as well have died because he is no longer in my life... sad but true. I had gone to Cairo to get more information surrounding his death. In the end, I know nothing more.

I've had enough. CJ had been my bud, my colleague, my source, my easy design answer. And when he got nothing—I got nothing. And I've got a big nothing now.

I'm going back—Pacific Ocean sunsets, the ocean, the sky, riding the surfboard, waiting for the next wave, waiting for design inspiration—just like I always did before CJ came into my life.

I've got two things to do—get back to my office and after work, hit the surf.

Illustrations

1-CJ's Voyages (also in front matter)

2-CJ's Arabian Home

3-CJ'sArabian Landscape (also in front matter)

4-Helvetia (also in front matter)

5-CJ Looks Inside

6-Grindelwald Bahnhof

7-Grindelwald View

8-Gletscherschluct

9-Malahide Hike

10-Grindelwald Bowl

11-Haybarns

12-Bree's Haybarn

13-CJ: Why Cairo?

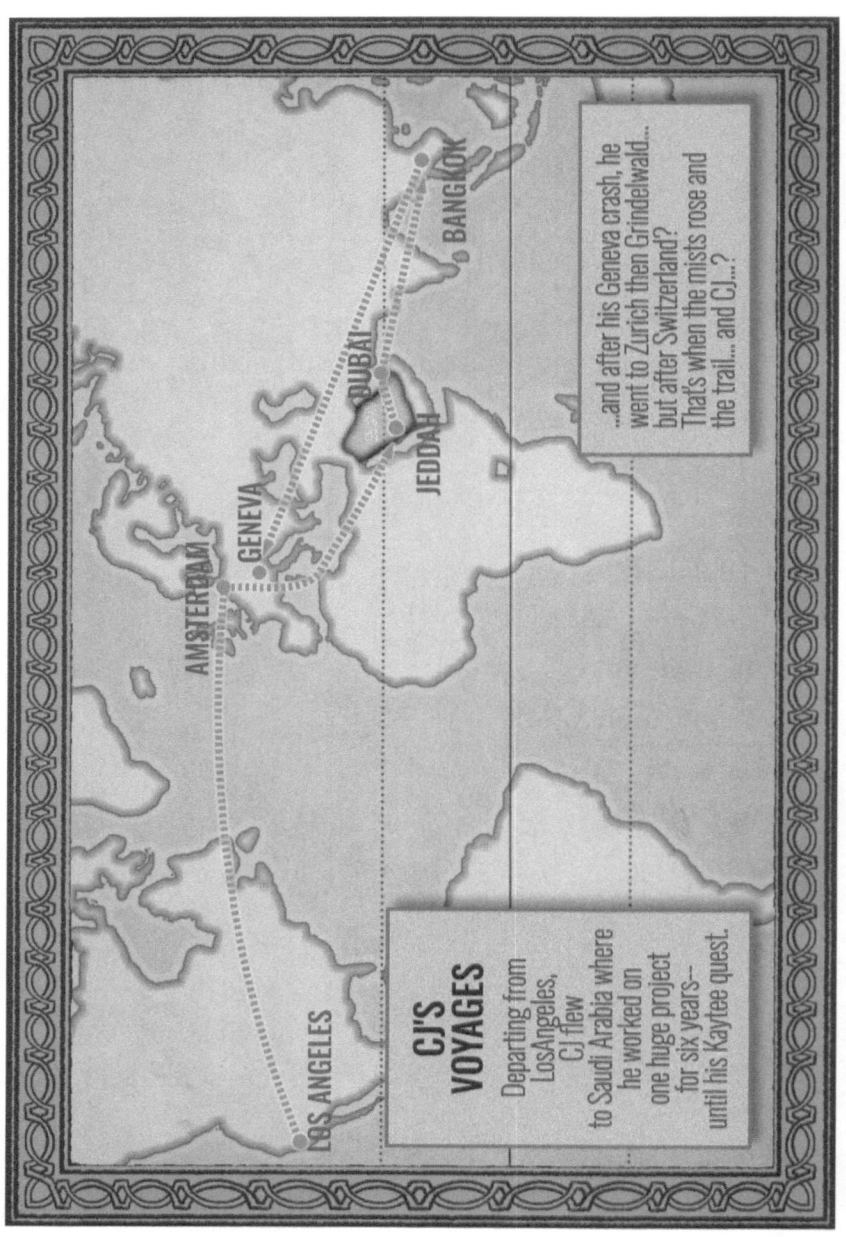

CJ'S
VOYAGES

Departing from
LosAngeles,
CJ flew
to Saudi Arabia where
he worked on
one huge project
for six years—
until his Kaytee quest.

...and after his Geneva crash, he
went to Zurich then Grindelwald...
but after Switzerland?
That's when the mists rose and
the trail... and CJ...?

LOS ANGELES

AMSTERDAM

GENEVA

DUBAI

JEDDAH

BANGKOK

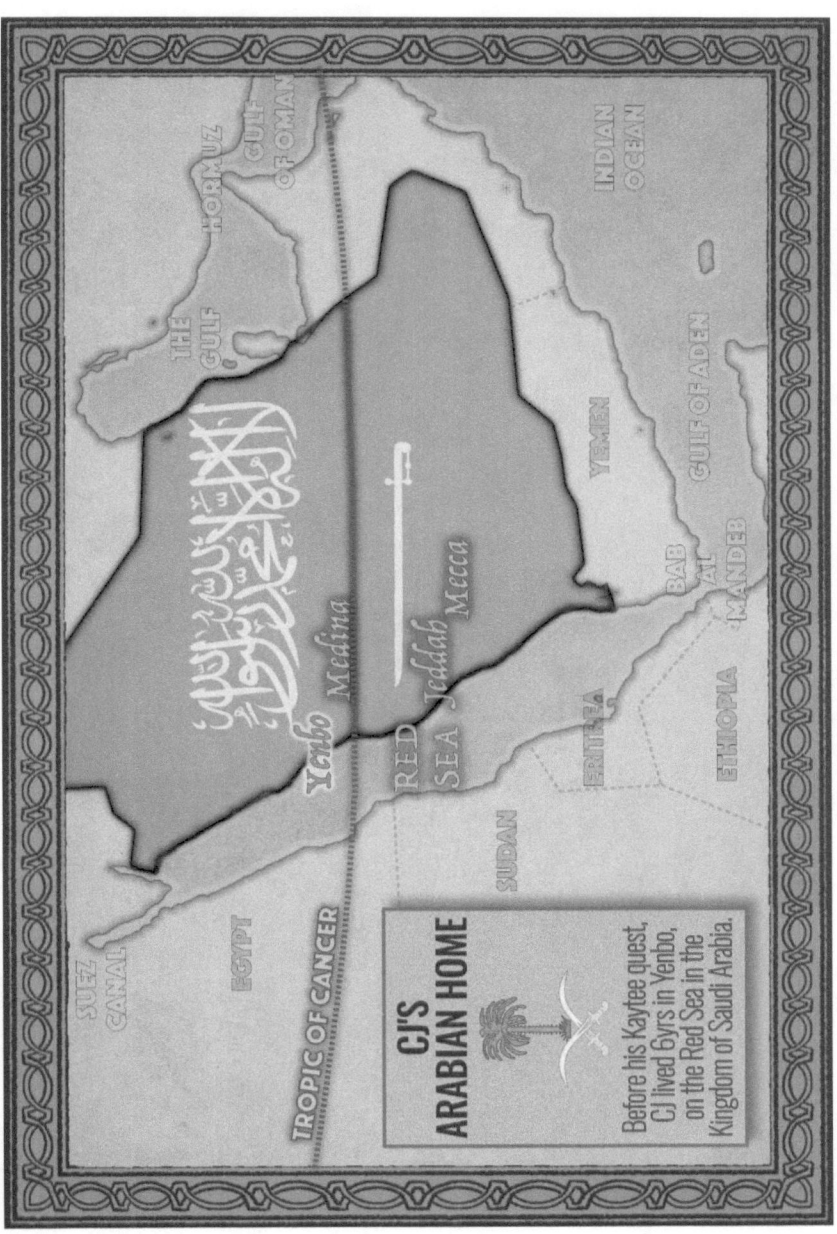

CJ'S ARABIAN HOME

Before his Kaytee quest, CJ lived 6yrs in Yenbo, on the Red Sea in the Kingdom of Saudi Arabia.

HIJAZ MOUNTAINS

TIHAMA COASTAL PLAIN

Yenbo

Mangroves and Coral reefs

RED SEA

CJ'S ARABIAN LANDSCAPE

Yenbo-40°Centigrade.
Salty sea,
sandy plains and
red ochre mountains.
Plants?
Mangroves and
coral reefs.

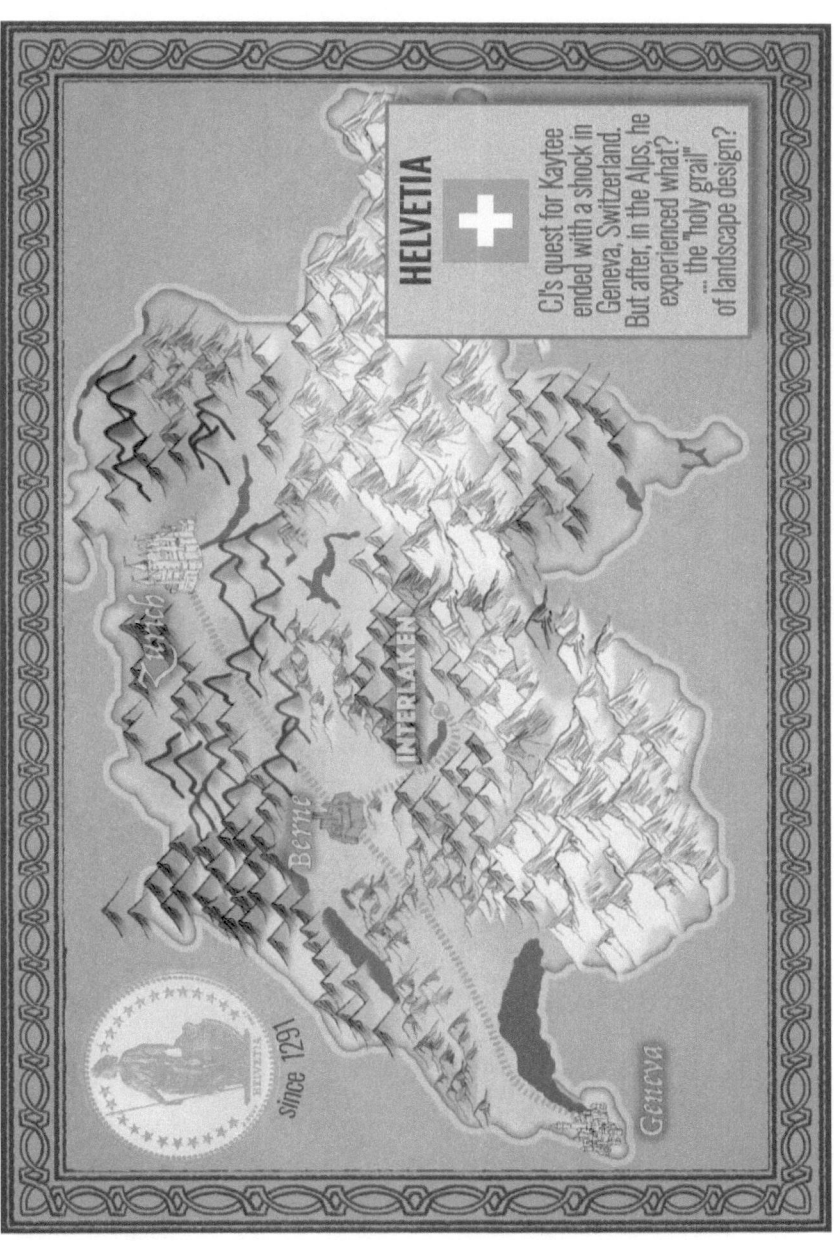

HELVETIA

CJ's quest for Kaytee ended with a shock in Geneva, Switzerland. But after, in the Alps, he experienced what? ... the "holy grail" of landscape design?

Zürich

INTERLAKEN

Berne

Geneva

HELVETIA

Since 1291

231

CJ rode the train from Spiez to Grindelwald. This Berner Oberland landscape, through its magical music, unravelled the "holy grail" mystery, enchanting CJ beyond words. Was this his "summum bonum" of landscape design?

CJ LOOKS INSIDE

GRINDELWALD BAHNHOF

Eiger, Shreckhorn and Wetterhorn dominate the Grindelwald skyline. Dwarfing the village, their cliff faces rise, from the edge of town, vertically a stupendous two kilometers.

GRINDELWALD VIEW

In the Berner Oberland, the Jungfrau Region mountains dominate the Grindelwald village which sits below and on the edge of a broad bowl filled with fertile pastures--the alps.

EIGER 3970

SHRECKHORN

GLETSCHERSCHLUCT

Grindelwald 1034

GLETSCHERSCHLUCT

In 1770, the famous naturalist and artist Casper Wolf painted the lower Grindelwald glacier pushing through a rock channel known as the Gletscherschluct.

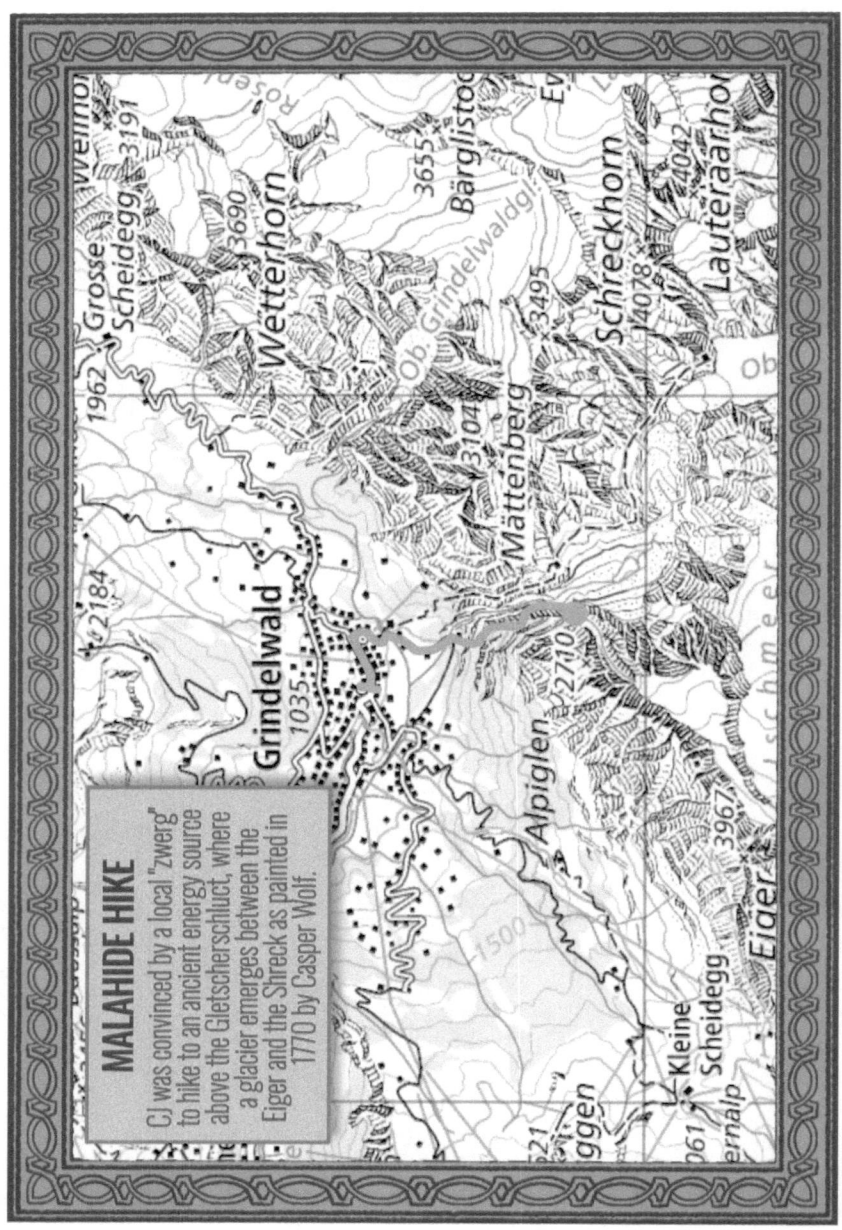

MALAHIDE HIKE

CJ was convinced by a local "zwerg" to hike to an ancient energy source above the Gletscherschlucht, where a glacier emerges between the Eiger and the Shreck as painted in 1770 by Casper Wolf.

GRINDELWALD BOWL

In the very bottom of this huge bowl of a valley sits the village of Grindelwald. Pastures (alps) and forests make up the rich soil landscape in this rain-blessed bowl.

HAYBARNS

Because the alps, the cow pastures, are in steep topography, the grasses flush out later and later the higher the elevation. Thus haybarns are essential for seasonal migration, grass feeding, cow milking and hay cutting.

To store the hay for the winter cow feed, the farmers build small haybarns sized for each of their small alps up and down the mountain slopes. The Berner Oberland haybarns are still built of salvage wood–a life of hard scrabble. And for Bree–the upgraded haybarn became her life, her plant world.

Bree used the gift from her Swiss grandmother to buy and upgrade the inside of a traditional Berner Oberland haybarn. From the outside it looked the same. But the inside and her gardens became the center of her life, her plant world.

BREE'S HAYBARN

1-Kitchen;
2-Private;
3-Stair to loft;
4-Botany;
5-Bookcases;
6-Campfire;
7-Gardens;
8-Forest.

CJ: WHY CAIRO?

Music, landscape and jobs have become his personal cocoons. And now? A new job in Cairo, the Sahara, and the world renown songstress from the countryside, Umm Kulthum.

THE SAHARA

EGYPT (MISR)

TROPIC OF CANCER

CAIRO

"The Landscape Architect" Series

In this Book 4, *Crystal Vision*, we learn how CJ, after six years in Saudi Arabia where he lost his job and his best friend, has embarked on a personal quest. That quest takes him deep into the Swiss Alps Jungfrau Region where, in the intertwining local culture and landscape, he discovers hope and a way forward.

The Landscape Architect series is about CJ, Christopher Janus. He wrote it all. The six stories are his collected memoirs. He was into asking questions, discovering and writing. And above all he was a landscape architect deeply intrigued by foreign cultures, landscape and design. The six stories track the arc of his beginning interest in landscape architecture followed by his growth in the profession.

Who is CJ? CJ is an American, born in the Midwest, raised in New Mexico—a hard worker who found his muse in the landscape. At university in the late 1990s he grew to embrace landscape, literature and all the fine arts with humanitarian, environmental and spiritual sensibilities. He became a landscape architect and despite his heart-felt attraction to the New Mexico landscape—inspired by the works of Ansel Adams, Georgia O'Keeffe, and the writings of JB Jackson—he travelled the world because, like it or not, life had its own plan for him. CJ's personal life and professional landscape architecture career are woven through with drama in landscape, foreign culture and design—all presenting him with unrelenting dilemmas.

The series reveals the twists and turns in his professional landscape architecture development. But the series explores further. CJ, drawing upon his fine arts history, becomes obsessed with experiences in nature and the landscape beyond the five senses. Beyond the five senses? The paranormal? He recognizes his limits yet is always striving to achieve more.

CJ chases nature, its landscape and plants to their existential roots. He describes his interactions with cultures, landscapes, gardens and plants of the world—where the unexpected and downright strange become daily facts of life.

CJ, like his landscape architecture profession and its practitioners, obsesses over design. In one of the major themes in the series, he tries to get to the root of the gossamer, ever-evolving landscape design theory. Unique in this series, CJ, not a tourist, uses his expatriate life across the Middle East, North Africa and Europe, attempting to weave the threads of his foreign landscape and cultural experiences into a pragmatic design theory.

Throughout his adventures and to his surprise, he discovers, on the good days, not the normal landscape architecture world, rather an enlightening and exciting ethnobotanical world influenced by the likes of Lord Byron, HG Wells, Algernon Blackwood and Rod Serling. And then there are the "not-so-good" days... strange cultures and even stranger landscapes.

Previously in Book 3, *Yenbo Palms*, CJ logically and successfully built his professional landscape architecture career in the United States only to be smashed by a huge personal disaster where he lost his wife and their three young kids in an horrendous automobile accident. That incident impacted him so deeply that his professional career was affected. Trying to forget, he ended up on a new town project for six years in the chimeric sands of the Kingdom of Saudi Arabia.

In Book 5, *Orient Espresso*, CJ is in Egypt, Vienna, the Jungfrau Region of the Swiss Alps, Istanbul, Bahrain, Kuwait and the United Arab Emirates. His professional career flip-flops—a combination of his own fateful choices and the capricious nature of international landscape architecture work in the Eastern Mediterranean and the Gulf Region.

First edition 2025

Final illustrations and cover art by copyright owner.

Edited and formatted by Lin White, Coinlea Services,
http://www.coinlea.co.uk

ISBN: 979-8-9851600-7-9

Published by copyright owner
https://flahertylandscape.com

Acknowledgements

All illustrations prepared by author. The illustration frames are Celtic themed from: Wonderdraft by Megasploot. Celtic? How deep can you imagine the landscape?

Base photos by author.

Base maps from 2022 Google Earth:

https://earth.google and from 2022 Swiss Topo: https://www.swisstopo.admin.ch/en.

The following illustrations base images have been provided in 2024 as listed below:

Illustration: 8-Gletscherschluct from:

https://www.zugerzeitung.ch/kultur/buch-buehne-kunst/caspar-wolf-der-pionier-der-alpenmalerei-ld.1649909

Illustration: 13-CJ's on his Way to Cairo from:

https://de.ethnicmusical.com/riq/Von-den-Pyramiden-bis-nach-Italien%2C-dem-Riq-auf-der-ganzen-Welt/

Colophon

Books are crafted. Colophons are the end credits of literature.

Books have a typographical tradition that to this author go nearly as deep into human culture as does the landscape.

Skia and Baskerville—both have roots and a clarity that befit Switzerland and CJ's landscape discoveries in the Jungfrau region of the Swiss Alps.

The end of each chapter is signified by the coat of arms from Grindelwald, the municipality that sits at the base of the world-famous Jungfrau Region landmarks (Shreckhorn, Wetterhorn and Eiger) of the Berner Oberland. Representing nearly a thousand years of recorded habitation, the blazon includes the seven alps/families/mountain communities in the municipality as well as a chamois, native to the area.

Cover Art

On this book's cover, upon examination, you will find a curated selection of cultural clues as found by CJ in the Jungfrau Region of the Berner Oberland, the northernmost range of the Swiss Alps:

1. Bobbin lace making, *klöppelstube*. Still active in the Lauterbrunnen Valley;

2. Wood from local managed forests for heating and for decorative chalet trim;

3. Gentians found in the Berner Oberland above 1500 meters in the pasture, the alps; and,

4. A five-franc Swiss coin.

All impacted Christopher Janus' landscape understanding while he was in the Jungfrau Region.

Dedication

Dedicated first of all to my wife, her photographs, support and understanding. Then to everyone who has interest in landscape, culture or the profession of landscape architecture.

About the Author

An international award winner and frequently invited conference speaker, Edward Flaherty practiced landscape architecture over the past five decades on very large projects where he has lived as an expatriate in Africa, Europe and Asia.

In Switzerland, he has been in the Berner Oberland with his family every decade since the 1960s. He is currently walking the Jungfrau Region.

Professional details at LinkedIn: https://ch.linkedin.com/in/edflaherty1

Discussion Guide for Crystal Vision

As I wrote this story, a couple big picture items kept me busy. I never fully resolved them, so I ask you, the readers, to discuss them and share your thoughts with me by commenting on my blog via this link: flahertylandscape.com.

1. Does human culture relate to the landscape? If so, then how?

2. What is the power in plants, gardens and landscape that induces peace in humans?

3. How do human cultures change? How do ecotypes in nature change? What happens at the edges of adjacent ecotypes and the edges of adjacent human cultures?

I look forward to hearing from you. Thank you.

Call to Action

Crystal Vision is the fourth book in the fictional autobiographical series, "The Landscape Architect". In the series, CJ tracks the intriguing events he experienced in his personal and expatriate professional career in landscape architecture amid the strange cultures and even stranger landscapes of Europe, the Middle East and North Africa.

If you enjoyed reading about CJ's *Crystal Vision* personal recovery, design and landscape adventures in the Jungfrau Region of Switzerland, then please write a short review and share it on my blog flahertylandscape.com.

You might also enjoy reading my third book *Yenbo Palms* about CJ's personal and professional adventures in the landscapes on the Red Sea in the Kingdom of Saudi Arabia, in Bangkok and Ban Muang Thailand and Geneva Switzerland.